DEVLIN'S CHOICE

by

HARRY F. KWARTLER

JAY STREET PUBLISHERS
New York, NY 10023

This novel is a work of fiction. Names, characters, places and incidents are either the product of the authors's imagination or are used fictitously. Any resemblance to actual events, locales, organizations or persons, living or dead is entirely coincidental and beyond the intent of either the author or publisher.

ISBN #1-889534-02-1

Jay Street Publishers
New York, NY 10023

SECOND EDITON - 1997

Manufactured in the United States of America

Front cover designed by Roy Horton

For
PEARL

ACKNOWLEDGEMENTS

I am grateful to the research staff of the Atlantic City Library at 1 North Tennessee Avenue for their unending support with local information and history; Bob Bishop, President of Title Agency of America for his vast insights into the intricacies of property ownership; The Lake Worth, Florida police for valuable information on firearms and general police methods; George J. Feneis for his technical advice on boats; Midge Boardman for her invaluable editorial comments, and finally to my faithful group of readers for their support and encouragement.

DEVLIN'S CHOICE

Chapter 1

"WHAT do you mean there's a delay? I cannot accommodate and I will not accommodate another delay. I just spoke to Langwell, down on Wall Street. If we don't wrap up the documentation within the next sixty days, there is a serious possibility of interest rate changes. The Fed is talking about upping the discount rate and if part of the two hundred million comes from abroad, who knows the cost of Eurodollars? Don't depend on the state passing the referendum to keep the rate down, even though my sources indicate it looks like it's in the bag. What's causing the delay, Addison?"

Addison Medford III hated to be the bearer of bad tidings. Especially to important clients. "There's a possible title issue."

"Oh, God! That's just what I need, another Battery Park fiasco!"

A tall blonde in a bright green dress, showing ample cleavage, rose from the floor behind Maxwell Zeist's chair and stroked the back of his neck. He waved her away, pointing to the photo gallery on the wall, displaying himself, "The Max," with the great and the near great, in various of his hotel holdings. She lingered. He covered the phone mouthpiece, kissed her cheek and whispered, "Go! Find the spot where your picture will be." Good. He was rid of the distraction. "What's the problem now?"

"They discovered a sliver of land, about fifteen feet wide. It lies close to The Palace Hotel, between The Palace and Caesar's, and runs from Pacific Avenue all the way to Boardwalk."

"Who knows about it?"

"Only my office and Joe Maddigan, the head surveyor for Atlantic City Engineering Co."

"Addison, tell me precisely what you mean when you say 'your office'? Who else knows besides you?"

"No one but myself and my secretary, Evie Conroy."

"Keep it that way. I'm paying your firm enough. Take care of it. Under no circumstances will I allow this two hundred million dollar financing to fall through. There's a fifteen percent Contingency Fund. Buy the damn little piece of dirt. The owner probably thinks it's worthless, but if you have to, spend a hundred thousand. You must get this problem solved."

"Vinnie Trentino won't like it if we touch one cent of the Contingency Fund."

Zeist gritted his teeth and ran a manicured forefinger over his thin hairline moustache. "I told you never to mention his name to me. I keep telling you, I never heard of him. Wrap this matter up, and do it within forty five days."

"And what do I do when Trentino, excuse me – your linen supplier, Brandywine Services, calls?"

"Screw him. I'll be in AC tomorrow, call me." He beckoned the blonde back to his lap.

Little Vinnie Trentino raced the Mercedes 600 SEL into the garage of the Chestnut Street building which housed Stern, Bradford and Altschuler, the largest law firm in Philadelphia. He usually sat in the back and let his bodyguard Stanislaus "Karl" Karlufsky drive, but in perceived emergencies, he controlled the wheel himself. He bounced over the speed barriers at breakneck speed, ignoring the shouts of the parking attendant. He impatiently cursed the elevator which arrived seconds after he pushed the "up" button. Then, charging past the receptionist's feeble attempt at a "Good morning, Mr. Trentino," he barged through the door of Addison Medford's private office.

"You said you would call me by Tuesday with the closing date. It's friggin' Thursday and I don't hear from you."

"Yeh, Thursday," echoed Karl, his glistening shaven bullet shaped head bouncing up and down on the massive neck of his hulking frame. Vinnie silenced him with a glare.

Medford nodded to his secretary. Evie Conroy silently rose from her dictation, smiled weakly at Trentino, her eyes seeking the floor, and discreetly left the room closing the door behind her. Medford meticulously arranged a stack of papers and toyed with the chess set on his desk, waiting patiently for his client to complete his tirade. He knew any interruption would be useless.

"I thought you and your bigshot, Zeist, had all the pieces put together. I give him the scratch to keep him out of bankruptcy. You tell me he has it in the bag with his Wall Street gumbahs; he gets his two hundred million from the bonds and I get mine out of the thirty million dollar Contingency Fund."

"Aside from the fact that you have incorrectly stated the transaction, Vinnie, please do not forget that The Max has been a substantial purchaser for all his hotel interests in Atlantic City. Linens, laundry, dry cleaning, food and only God knows what else, all from Brandywine Service Industries, the company I formed for you just four years ago."

"What the hell does apples got to do with oranges? We give service, we get paid. This is America, right? What the hell are you, Medford, a communist?"

"Yeh, apples and oranges," Karl giggled.

Vinnie turned to Karl with mock politeness. "Would you mind keeping your dumb Polack mouth shut while I talk to my lawyer. Thank you. Alright counselor, what's with my contingency fund money?"

Medford unhurriedly moved knight to KB-3, rose from his seat and answered his client. "Vinnie, let me refresh your memory and clarify any misunderstandings. This financing we are attempting to complete has a Contingency Fund under the Use of Proceeds section, in the approximate amount of thirty million dollars. That is not your money. The purpose of a Contingency Fund is exactly what its name characterizes. For contingencies. However, fifty percent of any unused portion, I repeat, unused portion, will go as a bonus to your investment company, Brandywine Capital, in addition to the return of any funds you have advanced to date. The remaining fifty percent will remain with Mr. Zeist. If, however, the Contingency Fund were reduced, because of any unforeseen needs, your bonus amount would also be proportionately reduced. That was, and still is, the deal!"

Trentino's face reddened with anger. He wiped the corner of his mouth vigorously with his thumb and leaned forward in a crouch, his powerfully compact, short body tightly coiled, poised to spring. Addison Grant Medford III, Harvard and private school graduate, the product of a cultured and sheltered upbringing, was riveted by the low, ominous voice. "Don't fuck with me, counselor. Tell me what's happening to my money."

"There is a problem. We cannot close this deal without absolute clear title. The Max previously had a title question on his New York City water front development. The financing went down the tube at the last minute. It cost everyone a fortune. Now the Wall Street syndicate won't touch anything that isn't one hundred percent approved by their title company."

"What the hell does that have to do with me? That's not my problem."

Medford enjoyed a crisis. He relished the opportunity to play the professor, to teach this uneducated hoodlum and his lackey the intricacies and vital importance of what he did. To show them, in clear calculating logic, how much they truly needed him.

"It's really quite involved. Let me explain it to you. An updated survey was required for the new financing. When this survey was completed, it showed that the point and place of beginning was different from the previous one. Possibly beach erosion changed it. Frequently surveyors use another surveyor's old work. In any event, there is a sliver of land that is not covered by our deed, and that could hold everything up."

It was the perfect place to pause, return his attention to the chess board, push a pawn and watch Trentino sweat. "Of course we could buy it. That would solve everything."

Trentino banged the table and jumped to his feet. Medford didn't flinch. "You wanna buy it, counselor, okay, okay. But don't figure on doing it with my money." He strode back and forth, cracking his knuckles rapidly, picked up Medford's letter opener, a small Arabic knife, that was lying on the desk, and ran the sharp edge along his finger. "Do you know who owns this – this sliver?"

Medford triumphantly raised the title report. "Of course. An old Atlantic City family named Tyler. I have the entire history and the name of the remaining heir. Or, I should say, heiress. It's a woman. I cannot approach her directly myself. My status as attorney would require some unwanted disclosure. I'll engage a stalking horse. There are many around that can serve my purpose."

"Awright, solve your problem, counselor. Like I said, it ain't mine." Little Vinnie motioned to Karl with a flick of his head. In seconds they were gone, leaving Medford's office door unshut.

Evie Conroy shuddered as they stormed passed her. This might be a timely opportunity to talk to her employer. Medford was a taskmaster who prided himself on putting in sixteen hours a day and expected the same of others. He made partner at twenty-eight, and now at thirty-four, was becoming a legend in the firm for how many employees he could fire or intimidate in any given thirty day period.

She and her husband had just bought a house in Wyncote. It was an old beauty but needed a load of renovation. She did her homework regularly. She had to. This was no time to join the ranks of the unemployed. It was the time to get a bonus. She went into Medford's room, the Tyler report in hand, and closed the door.

"Mr. Medford, I wanted to bring something and someone to your attention. You mentioned that you would want a third party agent to purchase the Tyler property. As a teenager I used to summer in Atlantic City. . . ."

"I'm not interested in your adolescent activities. Do you have something of consequence to tell me? I, apparently, unlike you, am very busy."

Silently, Evie bit her lip. "I believe what I have to tell you can be helpful. Margaret Tyler Crandell is the heiress to the Tyler sliver of land. I knew her when we were both teenagers – I'm only telling you this part, Mr. Medford, because you said you always wanted all the details. Dev, that is, Robert Devlin, has a small title company in Linwood. His secretary, Tess, and I are still good friends and I hear about him. Dev and Maggie, Margaret, used to be quite an item. If you wanted someone who could deal with her effectively, and possibly turn her head – well, he should be an ideal candidate."

Medford let his jacket fall open, tucked his thumbs behind his suspenders and permitted a rarely seen smile to cross his face. He nodded approvingly. "Very nice idea, Evie."

He pushed a pawn to queen 4. A small title company. He's probably a small, two-bit second rater. Let him run down a few blind alleys before he sees the Great Eastern report. Then he'll think he discovered America. If he can convince the Tyler woman that the piece has minimal value, maybe it can be bought for fifty thousand. It isn't easy serving two masters, but this is a place to do it. Be macho for the hoodlum and Max will love the coup. This should give me great leverage for a larger share of the year-end partnership profit split. He buttoned his jacket and removed the smile from his face. "Get me a report on him."

Whenever Dev walked into a casino his heart pumped a little faster. The same rush he felt going for the winning shot in a basketball game, or just before he broke the tape in the 100 yard dash. The vibes were good today in the Palace. He fingered the two fifties in his pocket. It was luckier to have two fifties than a single hundred, or five twenties. It's gonna be a perfect roll. Oh, great! Stan is working the box at my numero uno table.

"How you doing, Dev? I see you're wearing your lucky jacket." Stan pointed to Dev's old high school basketball jacket with its bold silver Mustang on a black background.

A wide grin spread over the cherubic black face of Billy Pierce, the stick man. "Hey, Dev, I hope you gonna be luckier today than you were in that last game in '74. Us AC Vikings beat your Mainland Mustang ass 114 to 92."

Dev smiled, gave Billy a two-finger salute and appraised the three players around the table, deciding which ones, if any, to bet with before it was his turn to shoot. He felt a tap on his shoulder and heard a soft feminine voice whisper in his ear.

"What's the matter, just because you're a James Dean look-a-like, you forgetting your friends?"

Dev shook his head, his attractive grin almost hidden as he looked down sheepishly. "Where you been keeping yourself, Jimmy? Got somebody else to dance with?" she asked.

Billy stroked the dice with his stick. "What are you talking about, Lorraine? That ain't Jimmy. That's Robert James Devlin. You see that jacket ? That man is still a star. Even though we screwed him to the wall ten years ago."

Lorraine continued, her gaze fastened to the silent

Devlin. "That doesn't impress me, Billy. He did that to me two months ago. Call me?"

Dev winked and nodded yes, as Lorraine drifted back to her spot behind the pit boss.

"Billy, you do not appreciate me," said Dev. "Your table was as dead as Kelsey's nuts. I made a special trip to come over and shill for you. You can't make any tips without action. Well, Billy my man, I'm going to give you a mountain of action and maybe win enough to buy this hotel from The Max."

Billy put his thumbs up for victory, his stick shepherding the dice toward Dev, rolling a five and two on top for seven and called, "New shooter coming out, a new lucky shooter, place your bets."

Dev dropped the two fifties on the table. Billy slid two even stacks of reds from the neighboring green twenty-fives, and the all powerful black hundreds, and placed them in front of Devlin. "Okay, baby, let's do it. Ten on the line, a dollar each crap-eleven and a dollar for my man Billy on the Eeeyoleven."

The red dice felt hot in his hand and the sound of the rattle sweet to his ear. He knew it, he felt it. He was going to run this hundred into a thousand. He was a winner, not like his old man. Come on, sweetheart, come on seven. He threw the dice slow and easy. They bounced off the back wall and landed, six and two.

"Eight, eight," chanted Billy, "the point is eight."

Dev stroked the chips in his rack and felt a small bead of perspiration roll down between his shoulder blades. "Place the six for twelve, put a nickel each on the five and nine and two bucks on the hard eight for me and Billy." His palm was damp as he lay it flat on the green felt. He twisted the pinky ring, turning the fading initial T downward and rubbed it three times for good luck. He placed the two fours straight up and along with the rest of the "do" betters, yelled for the hard eight. He rolled a nine. He pressed, adding from his winnings and the chips in his rack to increase his bets to ten dollars each. Eight, baby, give me that eight, come on you sweet double four. The dice flew in the air, landed in the corner and Billy called, "Eight, a pair of fours, Forty-four. He made it the hard way!"

He rolled seven or eleven four times and made the point three times. The "do" betters applauded; the win was building. Nothing could stop him now. Forget the thousand. He was going for five thousand, maybe ten. He had pressed all his bets, the money in the rack was down to twenty, but there was over seven hundred on the table. To his left, a heavy-set guy with a junket badge and a cap that had "Big Eddie" in red lettering across the front, had been betting black chips. Big Eddie was up over twelve thousand. A crowd had gathered around the table, drawn like a magnet to the shouting and screaming, and Billy's chants of winner! winner! winner! Dev was used to the crowds cheering him on. Just like the old days, the best of times.

The point was eight again. His favorite. He knew he was going to make it. He was sure of that. He was magic. This was the big one. He would repeat the hard way again. He closed his eyes and imagined the pair of fours as they would lay on the green table, the eight white dots staring up at him. He threw the dice slowly, gracefully, anticipating Billy's voice calling out winner! winner! winner!

A waitress tapped him on the shoulder, asking if he wanted a free drink.

"Seven and out, pay the don'ts and pay the last come. Thanks for the bet, Dev," said Billy.

Big Eddie counted his chips, paid off two of his markers, put a handful of blacks in his pocket and applauded. "Great roll, kid. Too bad the waitress jinxed you in the middle when she touched you."

"You win some, you lose some," answered Dev. He smiled at the cocktail waitress, threw his remaining chips on the table for the boys and walked out to the sunlit boardwalk.

Someone had pulled the plug out of the socket. He was drained. It was more than the money that was gone. Dev sank onto a bench, his head in his hands and stared at the fading grey herringbone weave of the Boardwalk planks. He slumped back and looked up to watch the strollers, walkers and joggers scurrying past him. Outfits ranged from cutoffs to Gucci jump suits. Some added rubbish to the debris-laden thoroughfare, ignoring the litter baskets next to the beach railing. He turned to observe the gulls doing their dance on the sand, prospecting for a reward with the same diligence he had seen in the senior citizens arriving on today's bus, fingering the slot machine wells, foraging for overlooked wins.

It was mid-day. The bright September sun hung high in the sky, competing with the neon brilliance of the flashing signs of Caesar's, Trump Plaza and Bally's. A tuxedo clad croupier sat down next to him. This guy looks familiar. His name tag read, "Ralph." Holy shit, it's Ralphie Caruso. We played basketball together in junior high. Heard he got a scholarship to some Ivy League school after he moved to Pennsauken. Good hook shot; he was a brain, too. What the hell is he doing dealing in the casinos ? He's so busy dragging on his cigarette he doesn't even recognize me. Damn butt smells good. Four months and seven days and I still miss the lovely weed.

"How you doing, Ralphie, long time no see."

Startled, Caruso dropped his cigarette to the boardwalk and looked up sharply. He appraised the face, scanned the jacket and chuckled. "Okay, okay. What the hell, I'm paying rent. How you doing, Dev? By the way, the ball game is over, you can take the jacket off now. What are you doing, coaching little league? Still working for your Uncle Bob? You're in real estate, right?"

"Not exactly. My Uncle Bob is in real estate. I got my own shop, a small title company in Linwood." I ain't going to wind up like you, Devlin thought.

"Great. Sounds a hell of a lot better than standing on

your feet all day busting your back dealing dice. I don't figure 'The Max' is gonna leave me the hotel in his will."

Caruso deftly gripped another cigarette with his teeth and pulled it out of the pack. Dev waited eagerly for the first burst of smoke to drift his way. "I thought your uncle was loaded. What happened?"

Devlin breathed in a last whiff of smoke and patted Caruso on the shoulder. "Someday I'll tell you." He rose quickly, disappearing down the boardwalk, deftly dodging the oncoming joggers.

Most of the locals call it New Road, but the tourists called it Route Nine. Devlin drove it every day on the way to his office, slowly rolling his black Corvette Coupe past the periodontist, chiropractors practicing their skills in tacky brown shingled free-standing buildings that looked like bungalows that might blow away in the next hurricane.

Dev's office was on a small side street at 190 Hamilton. Tess Donahue, his gal Friday, was the chief cook and bottle washer. Amid Tess, Darlene, a former cheerleader turned telephone receptionist, and Grace, the bookkeeper, Dev felt he was in a harem. And there were more females on the way. Tess was pregnant. It was going to be a girl.

Tess had her own room; the others were in the bull pen in front of his office which was down a short narrow hallway, insulating him from their conversations. In the back of the building, next to the bathrooms, was a warehouse area with ceilings twenty-two feet high. Records were stacked up to eighteen inches under the beams.

Along the back wall of Devlin's office, a row of trophies attested to his athletic triumphs; above them, opposite the window, were three shelves of old title records. On the wall next to his desk were the crayoned art works of his seven-year-old niece, Hayley, and her five-year-old brother, Alexander, children of his younger brother, Kevin. Kevin, the successful orthodontist, had been his mother's pride and joy, second only to her eldest, Danny, who had gone into the priesthood. Kevin had brought her grandchildren; Danny had brought her the solace of the church she needed to fill the vacuum of her marriage and the vagaries of her middle son, Robert.

Dev liked mornings best. Especially the silent ones. The coffee the girls made was mud. He could enjoy his "good coffee," eat the buttered roll still warm from the Greek diner and read the sports page of the AC Press before they drove him nuts with technical questions. He had his first sip when Tess walked in.

"Sorry, Dev, I hate to interrupt your morning ritual, but I think this may be important. My friend, Evie Conroy, works for a major Philly law firm and her bigshot boss is on the line. She recommended us. Do I get a commission for bringing in the work? You know I'm setting up a college fund for junior." Tess patted her stomach lovingly, pointed to the blinking phone line and left the room.

Devlin swallowed a mouthful of a roll, picked up the receiver, cleared his throat, preparing his voice for business like tones. "R.J. Devlin here, what can I do for you?"

He was greeted with chamber music followed by an announcement that someone would be with him shortly. Damn, damn, damn. He hated this crap. Next would be a dial tone and the telephone directory of the whole damn firm. That's the trouble with these big companies. You call in and get left sitting like a yo-yo office boy waiting for someone to show.

Evie Conroy's voice finally broke in. "Bobby Devlin, how have you been? Still breaking every heart in Atlantic County? I'm sorry I put you on hold, but I had to take another call before I connected you with Mr. Medford. Oh, wait, I see he just hung up. Let me connect you."

"Mr. Devlin, this is Addison Medford. I understand you do some title work in Atlantic County. If you are available, I have a relatively simple assignment that shouldn't take you too long and will pay a sizeable fee for the time spent. It involves a sliver of land that showed up. . . ."

"How big is sizeable, Mr. Medford?"

"Please don't interrupt 'til I'm finished, Mr. Devlin, I have an extremely busy morning. This sliver of land lies between The Palace Hotel and Caesar's. It's actually worthless to anyone because of it's shape. We prefer to resolve the question and not deal with its nuisance value."

"However, you do need it for clear title, right?" said Dev.

There was a beat of silence then a brusque voice responded. "Yes, we did elect to pay for it and give the title company a totally free mind on the matter. My secretary, Ms. Conroy, will give you the information we have to date and a letter of authorization to see any additional documents you might need. We're prepared to spend as much as fifty thousand for it, with an additional fifteen thousand as your fee to find the owner and make the purchase."

Dev drew in his breath silently. Fifty grand for a worthless sliver. And thirty percent for the acquisition. "Why me? I'm just small potatoes."

Medford smirked and could barely keep himself from laughing aloud. "Don't be so modest. Because we heard about you. You're the best."

Dev doodled fifteen thousand on the legal pad. He felt a rush. It was the race again. "How come so much of a fee?"

"Don't worry, you'll earn it. Get back to me with something in three days."

Chapter 2

TITLE records are kept in the county courthouse in Mays Landing. Devlin took Route 40 north past Rickels, Bradlees and the Clover Shopping Center. The stores kept popping up like weeds, changing the feeling of the area. Next year the NJDOT will probably remove all the old traffic circles that he used to practice on when he learned to drive. He knew two things would always remain. The old Jewish cemetery that Jake Balaban's family is buried in and the M&M Land signs.

He really didn't mind the drive. It gave him a chance to spend time in his 1991 Chevy Corvette Coupe. There were very few material things that Dev cared about and this was one. It was something he had wanted since the first time he parked one for a member at the Atlantic City Country Club. That one was red. His had a black exterior with black leather interior, six speed stick shift, 5.7 Liter V-8 fuel injected engine and could do 145 m.p.h. on a take-away. It cost him close to thirty thousand, had taken two years to pay off, but it was worth every cent to him. He called her the Black Demon. Tess teased him about the name. Devlin's Demon. She said it sounded like a Satanic cult.

The county clerk's office fronted on Main. The courthouse was erected in 1906. Its old red bricks were badly in need of pointing, but the windows, surrounded by brown steel shutters, could withstand an Indian attack. In April 1981, the Atlantic County government erected a statue to a Lenni-Lenape Indian chief. Local whites owned the county and, judging from the statue, all the chief got was a bag of wampum. Jake always complained there was never enough parking for him and the rest of the title searchers. Everyone had to go around the building to Second and Farragut. The Hamilton Township police parked wherever they wanted.

Dev crossed the new red brick sidewalk pavers, through the arcade of arches leading to the courthouse, past the metal detector gate which hopefully prevented any weapons from coming into the courtroom. He knew he would find Jake in the records room at the end of the hall on the second floor. He had to turn left; to the right was Criminal Records. Jake always complained like crazy about that. Jake ranted, every place you go, you gotta deal with some piece of crap that has committed a crime. This is not the way it used to be. In the old days, it was quiet, even though court was in session forty, fifty weeks a year and you didn't need a metal detector to keep the loonies out. There was respect for the law then.

The county had renovated the searchers' room about fifteen years ago. The old metal ceilings were gone, replaced by neon lights and acoustical tiling. Jake Balaban sat in his little booth, a courtesy from the county, paid for his own phone, got a spot to put his pads, pencils, stapler and do freelance piece work for Great Eastern and other title companies.

"Bobby, how do you like my newly renovated office?" he asked proudly, pointing to the picture of his twelve-year-old son. "Gimme a decent piece of work. David's going to be thirteen next April. We got to pay for the Bar Mitzvah."

"What I got isn't too involved, Jake, and there is a nice few bucks I can pass on. I need a title rundown on a small piece of land, probably a gore or a sliver that got missed in a survey when the metes and bounds didn't match up. Here's the description."

"Let's see what you got so far." Jake pulled at his thick, dark eyebrows and studied the file. A determined look covered his round face as he crossed the aisle to a row of record books behind him and quickly selected one. He muttered oy, shook his head and pulled three more. Dev had a fast eye, but Balaban was a speed reader and had almost total recall.

After two and a half hours of checking and cross checking, covering five pages of a legal pad with notes, Jake turned to Devlin with a knowing grin. "Piece of cake. Title was sold to four different owners in the last 30 years, most recently in 1955. According to Book 6243, page 1156, it now belongs to Murray Kleinerman. His address is. . ."

"I know his address. He's been running a salt water taffy shop since I was a kid. No problem. He'll sell it for peanuts. The guy loves the ponies, is always at the track. Dying for a few bucks almost as much as I am for a cigarette right now."

"You smoking again?"

"No Jake, just thinking about it. Thanks. That was dynamite fast. When I get paid, you get paid. Make sure I get invited to the Bar Mitzvah." Jake smiled proudly and nodded.

It was three o'clock when Devlin completed his file and left the searchers' room. He could call Medford now. No. It would be too soon. Let him think the midnight oil was burnt and he'll still be impressed that he got his answer within twenty-four hours. Devlin decided to return to AC. He could get there just in time to pick up Jack Devlin, Pop, at the Shamrock Pub and drive him home. Between the bullshitting and bragging of the deals he almost made, the old man should have had enough beer for one afternoon.

Years ago, Jack would have an occasional drink with

his future brother-in-law, Bob Vanderplatt, a Dutchman painter who bought an old house here and there, fixed it up, made some money and bought another one. Bob married Nora Kilpatrick, and Nora brought her sister, Maureen Anne Jane Kilpatrick, from County Mayo to the States. The Big Country, as they called it. She lived with Nora and Bob for three years, working as a domestic for the rich families in Margate and Ventnor. When she married John "Jack" Devlin, she hoped her husband would be the success that her brother-in-law had become in this grand, new land. Uncle Bob never went to the Shamrock anymore. He was too busy running his buildings, with the help of Timmy, his sister's, son. Nora and Bob had no kids of their own. Now Uncle Bob had Timmy, his own blood kin with him. That's when Dev left Uncle Bob. When Timmy came.

Dev took the Black Horse Pike towards AC, switching to the Expressway, which emptied out a few minutes from the Shamrock. It was a clear day, the bright sun reflected on the skyline, adding unneeded glitter to the names of Bally, Caesar's and Tropicana as he came closer to the city. The Trump Plaza Crest dominated the scene. He sped past the decaying apartment projects on Mediterranean, the laundry lines hanging visibly in front, a stark offense to the brilliant September horizon. Unkempt children played in the yard, casualties of unrealized dreams and unfulfilled casino and government promises. No wonder Mediterranean was always one of the cheapest Monopoly properties. Dev recognized the building where Billy Pierce grew up. Billy had his job dealing dice at The Palace, but will the rest of the Pierce family ever get out? Not a prayer.

At five-fifteen in the afternoon, the heavy flow of tourists and full time working regulars congregated at the Shamrock Pub. A small handful of the morning regulars, Jack Devlin among them, had lingered on. He had no steady job. A half-filled shot glass of scotch wavered in his hand behind the three empty Budweiser bottles arranged in a neat line in front of him.

"Hey, Pop," said Dev, "you're starting a little early on the hard stuff, ain't you?"

"Early, hell," yelled Jack's crony, Pete Banyan. "You're a little late today, Bobby. Your old man's already lost fifteen bucks playing darts."

"And no more drinks on the cuff, Jack," added Eddie, the bartender.

"That is, if he's got a shirt with cuffs left," someone shouted. The room rocked with laughter. They all knew Jack. This was funny. The big bag of wind was getting it from all sides.

Jack pulled himself up, leaning his slight frame against the table, his face red with anger. "Alright, you wiseguy son of a bitch. Who said that ? Which one of you said that? We'll see who hasn't got a shirt. I'll bet you – all of you, any one of you, fifteen – twenty-five bucks on a game of darts. One game of cricket. My son – my boy, Bobby, will throw the darts for me. This boy was a track star, threw the javelin – could have made the Olympics. That's right, the U.S. Olympics. Let's go, big talker. Mister bigshot. Come on, come on, come on!" He wiped the spittle from his lip and glared at them. "Alright. Let's see you put your money where your big mouth is."

The clink of glasses stilled. Devlin held his father by the shoulders to prevent him from falling. "Come on, Pop, let's go home."

Jack looked up, bleary eyed, touched his son's face, and whispered. "Do it, Bobby, do it. Do it for me and your mother, God rest her soul. Show them the Devlins can win."

No one came forth to bet. Jack sneered at them as Dev steadied his father's faltering stance. The bar conversation hushed and all eyes were upon Bobby Devlin as he walked slowly to the dart board. All that was heard was the overhead fan and the jukebox. Sinatra singing "Strangers In The Night." Dev pulled a dart from the board and rolled it in his hand. He concentrated on the target, focusing on the black rings surrounding the core, took unhurried measured aim, then quickly flicked his wrist.

"Great shot, great shot!" shouted Eddie. "Bull's eye! Dead center!"

Dev nodded to Eddie, stared at the onlookers, took his father by the hand and left. Jack held his head and muttered, "You're a good boy, Bobby."

"Yeh, I know."

He took Jack to the old house on Cheltenham Avenue, the one he had grown up in, now empty except for his father. Devlin wondered if Danny or Kevin would ever have gotten the call to take Pop home.

With his father settled in the house, he drove to his office on Hamilton Avenue, conveniently only a mile away. It was after five; the girls were already filing out; Grace, to pick up her husband; Darlene, hiking up her skirt on the way to a singles bar. Tess had remained to give him his phone messages. She held her back with one hand, and with the other, leaned against his desk to ease the pain caused by her extended stomach. "In case you want to call Medford, I put his number on your bulletin board. How did you and Jake make out today?"

"We made out great. Jake was a sweetheart; nailed it in one day. I was going to wait 'til tomorrow to call Medford, but I decided to do it now. I love to be the bearer of happy tidings and also pick up fifteen big ones. It's almost five thirty. Think he's still there?"

"According to Evie, this is still his morning shift."

"You look tired. You've been carrying a heavy load all day. Go home, lay back, put your legs up and relax."

"Great advice. That's how I got this way."

Devlin smiled, pointed to the door and silently mouthed the word "out." She slowly shuffled away. "Goodnight, I'm going. You lock up the store," Tess said, closing his door behind her.

Devlin dialed Medford's number, was put on hold to the strains of Vivaldi's Four Seasons. "What's wrong with Sinatra," he muttered, fumbled in his desk drawer for a hidden pack of cigarettes. He put one cigarette in his mouth, took a long imaginary puff and returned it, unlit, to the pack. The sharp voice abruptly interrupting the music startled him.

"Medford here."

"Bob Devlin here." He paused to catch his breath. Was it necessary to mimic the bigshot lawyer? Why do I always have to be such a smart ass? Guess it's in me blood, matey.

"Yes, what is it?"

"Bob Devlin, South Jersey Title. You asked for a quick response, so I'm giving it to you." One day, dammit, that was quick. He loved the hundred dash, the thrill of breaking the tape. Confess it, also of being the smart ass. "That sliver of land you're interested in, it's owned by a man named Murray Kleinerman. I know him personally and you should be able to get it well within your budget figures." Dev leaned back in his chair, put his feet up on the desk and smiled. No doubt about it, playing for big bucks with the big boys was cool.

Medford fingered the private investigator's report on Devlin he had read at six that morning. Robert James Devlin, age thirty-five, the middle son of John and Maureen Kilpatrick Devlin. Older brother, Daniel, a priest; younger brother, Michael Kevin, orthodontist. Well-known local athlete. High school and state records in track. Olympic candidate for javelin. No formal education beyond high school. Yes, he was popular with the locals, but Devlin conducted himself in the very manner that Medford had been taught to hate. He gambled, he went with loose women and, because of an insolent attitude, had lost two jobs. He doesn't know his place! My father is a judge and he is the son of servants.

"I contacted you because I needed someone to identify an owner and complete the purchase of a small insignificant piece of property. All you're giving me is stale news. We knew about Kleinerman a month ago. I thought when I hired you, I was getting the best. I must be overpaying. If you can't do better than that, I'll have to look for someone else." Medford heard no response. He smiled and pushed a pawn. The star, the people's hero must be squirming in his shabby office chair. "Well, Devlin, what's it going to be?"

"I'm sorry, Mr. Medford. I thought this was a good title rundown." Humble pie was not Devlin's dish, but fifteen thousand was dangling out there. "I promise I'll have something solid for you in forty-eight hours."

"You'd better."

That night, Devlin couldn't sleep. Losing was one thing, but looking like a jerk, a rank amateur, was another. And having to suck up to a pompous ass like Medford - God! At seven-fifteen he had finished his coffee and roll at the diner, read the sports page and the rest of the AC Press front to back. The editorial page had considerable comment on the public referendum being presented in the upcoming November election. If it were approved, the state would guarantee certain Casino Bonds, giving them a AAA rating. The referendum was strongly endorsed by three state senators and Governor Charles Everett Radcliff. Radcliff contended that casino support would add needed employment and revenues to the state. Radcliff was also up for re-election. His expenditures of campaign funds was the second largest in the history of New Jersey. The Press also noted that Maxwell Zeist, the major owner of Atlantic City casinos, lived up to his reputation of being "The Max" in his role as the maximum contributor to Radcilff's campaign. Dev tore out the article, underlined the section about Zeist and at the bottom of the page noted, The Palace–sliver – Medford–client?

He arrived at the office before the girls, left a note for Tess to call him at the Mays Landing courthouse if there was an emergency. He drove north on Route Nine, past St. Bernadette, the church that many gamblers waved to on their way to the casinos, looking for their own private miracles. He had promised Medford something solid in forty-eight hours. He waved at St. Bernadette.

Jake was in his cubicle peering over an old map of the district covering the convention center and Bally. The section including the sliver was traced on a separate sheet. Devlin tapped him on the shoulder. "Listen, Speedy Balaban, the report you whipped up in ten minutes made me look like a shmuck."

"I know, I know," said Jake "It bothered me all night. I didn't sleep a wink."

"You should have called me, we could have played gin."

"The whole shmeer doesn't make sense. It was too easy. Why would one of these lawyers, the very guys that always want us to work for peanuts, offer you so much money for what was really a nothing job ? In two seconds, Great Eastern would have known it. Any title company with half a brain could have figured out that Kleinerman owned it. So why would they do this," he murmured in a singsong chant, pushing his thumb to the sky, "unless, unless. . .unless they *knew* Kleinerman didn't own it because the real owner's name fell through the cracks." He stood, rubbed his back. "Come on let's go outside. It's stuffy in here. I'll buy you a coffee."

Abutting the court house, past the surrogate's office, was a small park with a green decorative fountain in its center, hundred-year-old oak trees and enough benches to accommodate the lunch time brown baggers. Jake sipped his coffee; Devlin spread the map of the hotel area; they leaned over it looking for a clue.

"Well, Balaban, you tell me. It looks pretty clean. How could it fall through the cracks?"

"A foreclosure."

"Come on, Jake. A foreclosure would just pass title. The new owner would be the high bidder. Title wouldn't fall through the cracks."

"True. But consider this, my friend. A survey is

taken from one point to the next; a sliver shows up because the point and place of beginning is different from one survey to the next. It could have started as a right of way. Maybe because beach erosion changed a starting point. Then, as you well know, Dev, the mistake is compounded in future surveys because so many guys use another certified surveyor's previous work. Right? Right! Now maybe the line is shifted over a bit, like a two or three foot strip across Boardwalk. Okay. Any one of these things could have happened, and then, poof, we wind up with a sliver, right?"

"Right. Thanks for the lesson, Jake, I know this stuff. Yes, we could get a sliver this way, but that still does not answer the ownership problem. A sliver is created, but who owns it?"

"Listen, listen. Why are you always so impatient?" Jake shook his head at his anxious friend. "Let me give you my theory. Think of the whole tract as a pie, and the sliver, a small slice in the middle of the pie. Now let's say the whole pie, the property surrounding this sliver is sold to some land speculator. Land speculators always need money, so let's say this particular land speculator goes to the bank and puts a mortgage on the whole pie. The bank wants a survey, and the surveyor *incorrectly encompassed* the sliver under the mortgage. Are you following me so far?" Dev nodded. "Next. The land speculator *doesn't* make the mortgage payments, and gets *foreclosed.* THAT'S THE KEY POINT. THE BANK NOW HAS THE DEED ON THE WHOLE PIE! AND THAT IS HOW THE DEED AND THE OWNERSHIP TO THE SLIVER IS ERRONEOUSLY PASSED.

"You see, my impatient young friend, when the sheriff completed the foreclosure sale for the bank, he improperly transferred the sliver, which never should have been encompassed in the first place. The Kleinerman family, their lawyer and surveyor, thought it was included when they purchased the land and buildings where the taffy shop is. The wrong party thinks they own something they do not.

Bingo."

"Very interesting theory. So tell me Rabbi Jake, why doesn't Great Eastern or my big shot Philly lawyer know this?"

"Maybe they do, maybe they don't. Why would they call you if they knew?"

"You always answer a question with a question. Seems to me what we need now is a title company with maps that go back to year one. Where do we go for that?"

Jake shook his head and shrugged his shoulders. They sat in silence, watching the pigeons collecting yesterday's lunch scraps. Next to the fountain, a young couple embraced and kissed. Jake nudged Dev, pointed to them, then suddenly smacked his forehead.

"Title Agency of America. One of the searchers told me they bought all the maps and files of Sea Land, after Sea Land went bust. Sea Land had every old map in Atlantic County. Maps that had never been recorded in the county clerk's office. They might have this section." Jake rubbed his hands, stood quickly and did a small jig.

"Hey Jake, just looking at those young kids necking got you so excited? I'll buy you a couple of pornos and you'll be ready to buy out Great Eastern."

Jake shook his head disapprovingly. "Wait here. I'll go across the street to the Rexall, call Al Richman at TA and see if they have it." He loped to the corner, eager to be assured that he had, indeed, solved a difficult problem.

"Jake," Dev called, "don't buy a copy of Playboy. Arlene will kill you."

Jake waved Devlin's words away and disappeared into the drugstore. Dev stared at the building, remembering it as a local landmark for almost a hundred years and hoped it didn't collapse today. Jake appeared, gave him a thumbs up sign, and pinched his own cheek.

Chapter 3

TITLE Agency of America was the second largest title company in the tri-state area. Great Eastern was first. TA had eighty five employees and a warehouse area of over twenty-five thousand feet to store records and maps. It had started with his wife's family, but Al Richman had built the business to its present size. It was his idea to buy Sea Land's old maps and files because he thought it was smart business. He was a small bald man of sixty-two who hated to be pushed around. These files gave him an edge. He also pursued collecting the history of the county. His family had founded the old Atlantic Journal, the first newspaper in Atlantic City. He loved Jake Balaban. Jake was, to him, a true student of the art of title searching. Al gave Jake work whenever he could. They respected one another.

Dev was greeted warmly after Jake's phone call. Within minutes of his arrival at TA, he found himself in the rear of the warehouse where Sea Land's maps were. The air was heavy with the musty smell of decaying paper and chemicals. Worn purple leather bindings surrounded deed books with mottled surfaces. Torn pages hung loosely off the edges, rustling with any movement, like the skin of an old man. Dev tripped on a step ladder used to reach the upper shelves, sending bits of broken, aged parchment fluttering toward styrofoam covers of the computer boxes. Old and new record keeping had merged. He found a map of the

Brigantine inlet and Atlantic City, dated 1899. There was no development in those years. It started later on Ventnor Avenue, in small tracts, then stopped, leaving nothing but vast open spaces inland, uninterrupted to Pleasantville. Countless volumes with loose threaded canvas covers, awash with algae swimming between their pages, were piled on racks that reached to the ceiling, a silent testimony to the past.

After two hours of searching, he stopped at an old, tan map cabinet, its flat surface etched with rust. It contained layers of surveys, dating back to 1840. In the third drawer he found a map of the Absecon inlet. The legend read, *"The Division of Lands of Jeremiah Tyler."* The division showed lands, described by deed, going from Jeremiah Tyler to Joseph Tyler, dated June 23, 1843. At the end of the division was a tract where the sliver would have been. This was the date and section for which he had looked.

Maybe the files were bunched? Another small ladder stood in the aisle next to the cabinet. Dev carefully climbed the six steps and found the adjoining maps of the sub-division. It included that entire section of Pacific Avenue and St. James. Underneath the maps he found Book A, the first book in Atlantic County, dated 1839. He raced his fingers along the title transfers. It was there. The complete description. It was still in a Tyler name. The surrounding lands had been sold to new owners, but the sliver had passed down over the years, always remaining owned by the Tylers. Jake was right!

Maggie Tyler Crandall. If this *was* Tyler land – *is* Tyler land – then it belonged to Maggie. Or, since her mother died, to her son-of-a-bitch old man. No. Maggie had said any Tyler land always stayed with Tyler blood. Good. Better to deal with her than Jonathan Bishop Crandall. Oh, Maggie. He said her name aloud. After all those years. He had never forgotten her. He had compared every woman he had been with in the past seventeen years to her. To Maggie's golden beauty and a voice that entranced him. It was going to feel strange calling her now. After they had agreed not to meet, not to speak.

Devlin looked at his watch. He didn't need forty-eight hours. He would give the Philadelphia lawyer a solid answer in less than twelve. Dev thanked Al Richman for his courtesies and was advised he could make any phone calls from the small office off the reception area. Richman sent his best regards to Jake.

Calling Medford's office was always an experience. The firm had one hundred and twenty partners; speaking to someone directly was a nightmare. All a caller got was frustrating instructions on how to use voice mail. After the second detour, he heard a human voice.

"Evie, it's Dev. Connect me with the Pope. I found the holy grail."

"Hold on one sec, he's on with a major client. Don't go away; I'll shove a note under his nose." Devlin listened to the beginning of Mahler's ninth. "Thank you for waiting Mr. Devlin, here's Mr. Medford."

"Well?"

"Mr. Medford, I promised you quick action. I'm a man of my word. . ."

"I'm busy. After you've finished congratulating yourself, tell me what you have."

Devlin inhaled softly, suppressing himself from telling off this blowhard. "The sliver of land you're interested in is owned by the Tyler family. I can supply you with copies of the maps and the analysis of my title report tomorrow." Devlin heard no response from the busy man, but thought he heard someone clearing his throat.

"It's quite a coincidence that you called me just now." Medford shifted gears quickly and smoothly. So, the second rater came up with the correct title information without being helped. Interesting. "We were going to call you. I just received a report from Great Eastern confirming this exact information. Now finish up the good work as discussed."

"I don't know if that is going to be possible. The

Tylers are one of the oldest and richest families in the county, so you may have to adjust your thinking on the price."

"They *were* one of the richest families. It seems that Jonathan Bishop Crandall, the gentleman who married Ellen Tyler, lost most of the family fortune in some very speculative investments. They have a daughter, Margaret. It is her inheritance."

"I know her."

"Good. You seem to know everyone in the county. Obviously when we hired you, we did hire the best. As for the price, I think you may not have too much difficulty with the daughter. We are advised that she's returned to the family home. She has separated from her husband and also may be in need of funds. I'm sure you can properly explain that the sliver has very little value. Call me no later than Friday."

The phone went dead in Devlin's hand. He grinned at it. Counselor Medford, you really should call Miss Manners. You just *never* seem to say goodbye.

Dev started back to his office. Maggie Tyler Crandall. Wonder what her married name is? After a mile on the White Horse Pike, a sudden impulse sent him toward the ocean. He met Maggie in '74. He worked the beach as a lifeguard that summer, at the South Carolina and Tennessee station, where all the local high school kids hung out. The ones from Holy Spirit, AC High, and Mainland, his school. The beach patrol captain gave him plenty of room. Once Rebecca King, Miss Colorado who became the 1974 Miss America, took a public relations photograph there for the papers. She asked him to be in it. Right next to his stand, with Central Pier in the background.

Maggie had never gone to his beach before. She was a Tyler. She didn't hang around with the locals. She went to Pilgrim Academy, the fancy private school in Galloway. But, that one day, the day that Evie had the visiting out-of-town cousin who wanted to see Central Pier, the three girls decided to go slumming and spend the afternoon with the peasants. Down at his beach. The local girls pointed at him. He was a celeb, the hot shot athlete. Everyone knew Dev.

It was Evie's cousin who decided to talk to him. Maggie was shy, but went along. He didn't look at the cousin or Evie. Maggie's golden hair and long legs commanded his view completely. Many pretty girls had admired him. Their attention was not unique. But she was. She had the most appealing way of smiling, and then becoming embarrassed by its very beauty. Their gaze met and they crossed a silent bridge of understanding. It happened so quickly. It changed their lives.

She came to his station every Saturday for the rest of the summer. When his shift was over, they would walk, hand in hand, down the beach as far south as Providence Avenue, where the Golden Nugget would be built one day. Past Pacific and a sliver of land that would bring them back together again. Maybe not together, but at least to meet again.

It would not be like the meetings of the old days. They had come from two different worlds. Dev from a middle class Irish family, his mother just one step off the boat, his father but two, was brought up in a small house in Linwood and had worked since he was fourteen. Margaret Tyler Crandall was the great-great granddaughter of Jeremiah Tyler, one of the earliest settlers of Absecon Island and for many years the single largest land owner. She had attended private schools since she was born, had gone abroad for the first time at the age of ten.

Young Maggie's home, at the corner of Atlantic and Thurlow in Margate, was not her first home. It was one that her mother, Ellen, had later chosen to be near the Margate Community Church. It was a colonial brick house, with fourteen rooms. One room, on the top floor, with a clear view of the church spire reaching to the sky, was a refuge for Ellen, to give her comfort from the tensions often caused by her husband.

The location of the Atlantic Avenue house proved to be a godsend for Maggie's secret meetings with Dev. Lucy, the Margate elephant at Decatur and Atlantic, was only a few blocks away. Lucy was open until Labor Day. Maggie didn't need a car for the quick, easy run on a summer night, the stealthy climb up into Lucy's howdah and Dev's arms.

Her father didn't approve of him. The Devlins were low class provincial. This boy parked his car at the Atlantic City Country Club. Jonathan Bishop Crandall made it very clear that his daughter should not pursue any friendship with hired help. But she did. Dev would be waiting, leaning on the iron fence in front of Lucy or in the refreshment house. On nights when she couldn't escape, the beach lookout stand was an agreed drop for notes to be left with his friends for a future contact. The Greenhouse cafe, next to Lucy, was only a shack in those days, but it was an ideal place for a drink, a smoke, a grab under the table, praying to god the old man wouldn't catch them.

Dev remembered their first time. He had vowed never to return to her house again after Jonathan Crandall had called him Irish trash. Maggie had called, her voice a whisper. Come to me tonight. Her parents had gone to a wedding in Baltimore. He parked the car on Union and walked around the corner to Thurlow. She had left the key in a small enamel pill box in the bushes. He found it, silently climbed the stairs to discover her waiting for him in her bedroom. The sight of the moonlight streaming through the window, silhouetting her long legs under her thin night dress took his breath away. It was more consuming than either expected. She was seventeen. Still a virgin. He wasn't surprised. Their love making continued through the summer and into early winter. Who thought it would end so badly, with a promise never to see one another again. Now they would meet again. But this time it was different. It was strictly business.

The Franklin Bank & Trust Company was the oldest and largest institution of its kind in the state. It was not the largest bank, but it did have the largest trust department. FBT had represented the Tyler family for one hundred and forty years. Stern, Bradford and Altschuler was the bank's primary law firm. Medford's contact at Franklin was Richard Murdock, his former Dartmouth roommate. When he needed something, Medford made the calls personally. It was a good contact. Medford had gotten him the job.

"Rickie, I need a small favor. I'd like to review all of your old Tyler documents. It's not important, but it might save me some time on a title matter. I'll send someone over for them tomorrow. Have them ready by ten."

Murdock snapped the pencil in his hand. He doesn't ask, he just demands. "Addison, the Tyler files go back for over a century. It would take a month to decide which ones to give you. And they *are* private papers."

"Rickie, Rickie, don't get so up tight. I just have to clear a small title question. I'm not prying into personal or historical papers. Let me look at old deeds and wills. You know, the kind of document that would have been filed in the county clerk's office anyway. Who knows? In those days, some papers just weren't recorded. You'll take care of that, won't you? Good. Let's meet and play squash next week. The papers, tomorrow at ten."

He was superstitious. At times he felt lucky going into the casino, confident of a win, the same way he felt in the old days, sure he was going to win the race. Other times he was unsure. It was not smart to push the Fates. Dev sought out the old pay phone on the boardwalk. The one he had used to call Maggie. It would be lucky to use it again today. Damn! A new one had replaced it. He looked for her initials on the wall, where he had scratched them a lifetime ago. Another vanished talisman. He remembered the number easily. That was indelibly etched; time could not wear it away. His heart beat wildly, anticipating the exquisite music of her voice.

"Hello."

It came through like a crystal bell in the darkness of his clenched eyes. "Hello." Yes, Maggie, Maggie. He remained, eyes closed, suspended, recalling her image, overlooking the need to speak.

"Hello."

"Maggie. It's me, Dev. How are you?"

Now it was her turn to feel her heart in her stomach. "Dev, I can't believe it. How good to hear your voice. I'm fine. Well, pretty good. How are you? I heard about your mother dying last year. I'm sorry, I know how much you loved her. I know how it feels. I almost called you."

"Yeh. Thanks. And I'm sorry about your mother too. Were you really going to call me?"

"Yes, Dev. Is that why you are calling me now?"

"No, Mag. I never called before. You know that. I kept my promise to your father. Actually it's about business. It concerns a small piece of land your family owns. That you inherited, I guess. Can we meet?" He held his breath. Why doesn't she answer me? Come on, Maggie, say something, anything. I can't stand this.

"Of course we can meet. I don't care anymore about the promise to my father. We're old friends, and you said it's business. I would love to see you. Most afternoons are okay. I do interior design work and I'm usually free by two or three. Except, I can't tomorrow. Any day but Wednesday. "

"How about Wednesday?"

"Oh, Dev, Dev, I see you haven't changed. Still the charmer and probably as handsome as ever." She laughed softly. "Okay. Tomorrow." That voice of hers. It blew him away.

"Great. Wednesday at three. How about the Greenhouse Cafe. It's near your house, remember? And one other little favor please. Wear a ribbon in your hair."

Maxwell Zeist rarely went to the offices of his attorneys. They usually came to him. He had numerous law firms representing him in five major cities in the U.S. and one in London for his international work. Primarily financing.

This week he was in Philadelphia for a public relations promo. He spent the morning on Market Street being photographed in front of the Liberty Bell with Jessica Lee Andrews, Miss Pennsylvania, the favorite to win the Miss America pageant. The next photo session would feature Jessica and "The Max" at The Palace Hotel. People Magazine would feature the story. There was an hour and a half break between photo sessions. Zeist didn't like to wait. But this might be a profitable delay. Channel 3, KYWT, the local NBC affiliate, would cover the story and take it national. Maybe CNN would pick it up. "The Max" never passed up opportunities for media exposure. He used the remaining free forty-five minutes with Medford at Stern, Bradford & Altschuler.

They met in the Chinese Room, an intimate conference room, the smallest of the four, tastefully decorated with Chinese art, wall hangings and one screen that cost more that most of the secretaries made in three years. Zeist was the only client permitted to smoke in this room. He enjoyed his Havana cigars, but he also admired the art and rarely abused the privilege. He rolled the Havana between his fingers, brought it to his nose and inhaled the aroma.

"Max, we have a wrinkle in the sliver business," said Medford.

"I thought you had everything under control ! What's the snag now?"

"Well, it's not exactly a snag. Some might consider it an opportunity. I happened to come across some papers that were at Franklin Trust which shed new light on the matter. There is an old will."

"So? You mean it's not owned by that old family – Tyler ?"

"On the contrary. It definitely is owned by the Tyler family. Just a question of which one. I'm no longer in possession of the original will, but Evie Conroy has made a copy for me. I've written a synopsis of the pertinent points. Let me read them to you."

Zeist extended his hand, motioning for the papers. "I'm a speed reader, Addison, and I prefer to see the written word."

Medford handed them over, piqued at the lost opportunity to play the pedant. Zeist swiftly scanned the pages, chortled, put the document in his lap and returned to his unlit cigar.

"These Tylers were a very interesting family. Different sense of morality, but of course those were different times." He chuckled again. He was feeling very expansive. "Thank you for showing this to me Addison. We might be lucky and get the sliver of land for less, but don't stop trying to buy it. We *must* close on it. Especially with the referendum coming up. I told you before, spend what you have to. Don't hesitate to use some of the Contingency Fund."

"I intend to. But I also represent Trent – other clients. I may have to disclose certain elements of this will."

Zeist shrugged, lit his cigar and blew a perfect smoke ring towards the two hundred thousand dollar oriental screen.

Maggie finished her work at the Drexel School of Design and was ready to leave Philadelphia early enough to make that extra stop before her meeting with Devlin. It was a meaningful stop. Especially today. She drove through Linwood, past Mainland High. Perhaps she might be blessed with a glimpse of Sara. Even a fleeting one. Maggie hadn't enjoyed much more than that from Sara over the past seventeen years.

She drove around the school slowly, timing her visit to the hour when students came out for their gym period. She parked on Monroe Avenue, overlooking the massive athletic field. In the background, under the big M and the Mustang, the stands stood empty. She filled them with the memories of her youth. The remembrances of herself, Evie and the crowds around them, all chanting, "Devlin, Devlin, Devlin," spurring him on to victory.

There was no sign of Sara. Time to return to the present.

The Greenhouse Cafe, once a modest hangout, was now sleek and modern. A large glass porthole window faced Atlantic Avenue with bold scripted, green lettering displaying the name. A banner across the front door disclosed it was under new management. She was early. Ten to three. Uusally late, he already was there, waiting for her,

He stood quickly, awkwardly for someone whose movements were routinely marked with grace. They approached tentatively, uncertain what the rules were. To extend a hand? To kiss? They embraced lightly. Doubtful, without passion. Yet, when he held her, the perfume – what was it? It still held a spell. He felt her tremble in his arms. They stepped back and sat at a table.

"Can I buy you a drink?"

"No, no thank you. Wait. Yes, I'll have a glass of chardonnay."

He ordered a bottle of Heinekin for himself. "So, how have you been?" She shrugged her shoulders and shook her head side to side. Noncommittal. "How long has it been, Mag, sixteen, seventeen years ?"

"Seventeen years, four months."

"Yeh, I know," said Devlin. He checked his pockets for a cigarette. "You smoke? No, no, that's right, you never did. I quit." They sat in silence. He traced the square table cloth design with his finger. "Heard you got married. Did your old man like this one? Anybody would have been better than me, the mick lifeguard. Isn't that what he used to call me?"

"Dev, please. I'm separated from my husband. Is that why we're here? To discuss my unsuccessful marriage?" She had acquired some of her father's aloofness along with his patrician good looks, the wall of coolness rising quickly to protect her invaded privacy.

"No. You're right. I called you because of a small piece of land you inherited. I've been hired to find the owner. I did, I found you. Next, I'm supposed to buy it for my client. They authorized me to offer fifty thousand dollars."

"Fifty thousand dollars? I could certainly use the money. Especially now. About the price – I have no idea as to value. You said it's a small piece. How big is it ?"

His answer was instantaneous. "Actually, it's only a sliver, probably not worth the offer." Devlin flushed in his betrayal. You Judas! Has Medford got you in his pocket for the fifteen thousand?

Maggie had heard about land transactions all her life, since she was a child on her grandfather's knee. "If it's only a sliver, why would they pay so much?"

"Because of its location. It's between two hotels, near Boardwalk. The lawyer didn't disclose his client's name, but I've got an idea who it is."

"I've already admitted it, Dev. I need the money. Should I take it? Am I making a mistake?"

This was more than he had bargained for. She needs fifty and he wanted the fifteen. My God, Dev, this is Maggie, She's pressed for money. He couldn't take his eyes off her. She had matured. She was gorgeous. It was getting easier. "I think you should hold out for more."

She smiled. "I'll take your advice. But I'm not quite sure how much more." They sat in comfortable silence, inspecting one another, seeking the familiar. "Is this what you do for a living? How did you get into it?"

"You remember my Aunt Nora, the one I told you who brought my mother to the U.S.?" Maggie nodded. "Her husband, my Uncle Bob – I was named for him, well, they never had any kids so he took me into his office and taught me the title business. I figured one day he would leave it me, at least until Timmy, his sister's son, came to work there. Timmy and I got into a little argument one day. I broke his nose."

"Oh, Dev. You always did have a hot temper. Your uncle fired you?"

"Well, he started giving me this lecture about his side of the family, and blood being thicker than water. So, I quit. Two weeks later I started my own company. That was seven years ago."

He placed his business card on the table and pushed it to her. The crisp lettering was easy to read. South Jersey Title Company. R.J. Devlin, President. He grinned with boyish pride.

"About your sliver of land, there's something I want to check before you counter offer." She looked at her watch. "I know, I know, you've got to go. You always had to live by the clock. I'll walk you to your car. Did you park by Lucy ?"

They stood by her car in front of the great Elephant, hesitant of the farewell. Meetings and partings were new to them again. Before she left, he knew he would ask her. He had to.

"When did you do it?"

"When did I do what?"

"Maggie, don't play games. You always said I was the one that played too many games. You once told me that what went on between us was just another game to me. It wasn't. Tell me, when did you do it? Where did you go to have it done?" Her eyes slid from his. She did not answer. He controlled his urge to shout. She had to tell him. Yes, he had a temper, at times uncontrollable. He would not be left in the dark any longer.

"Come on Maggie, jog your memory. It wasn't an event we didn't talk about. You mean you forgot, when you weren't even eighteen you were pregnant? You mean you forgot I was the father, but I had no say in what was to happen?" She started for the car door. He grasped her arm.

"Who the hell would listen to me! I was the nobody who parked your father's car at his fancy country club. I was just the mick lifeguard, not good enough to set foot in your house. I sure as hell always remembered that. But your old man says, if I promise never to see you again, or speak to you again, he'll take care of everything. He'll let me off the hook."

Devlin banged the top of her car with his free hand. "Let me off the hook. I'm spilling my guts out every night, crazy in love with you, and he'll let me off the hook." Devlin's face and strength drained as he loosened his grip on her arm. His voice was low and small as he continued. "And you tell him, it's okay. That's what you want. You'll do it. You'll do what your father says. So, you go for the abortion, off to college and out of my life."

Devlin stepped away, desperate for distance. He looked up at the sky and rubbed his eyes hard. "Did I leave anything out?"

Maggie got into the car and brushed the tears from her cheeks. "Actually, Dev, you left out a lot. But it doesn't matter, it's the past. I don't want to talk about it anymore."

He picked up a rock and threw it toward the ocean. "Okay. We'll drop it. I'll take care of your business. Don't worry, I'll get you a great price, Mrs....what did you say your married name is?"

"I kept my maiden name."

He turned his eyes from hers, and faced the ocean again. "You should have kept me instead."

Chapter 4

DEVLIN didn't go home. He was unsettled from the meeting with Maggie. There was something that wasn't right. A nagging thought told him to check the sliver location. He drove north to the boardwalk in front of the spot where he calculated the sliver was located. There, he unrolled the map from Title Agency of America and spread it out on a bench. It was six o'clock, the setting sun cast a golden glow over the ocean, shedding enough light to read the survey lines.

He paced off measurements and estimated the distance from the southerly side of The Palace Hotel. Zeist owned The Palace. Devlin patted his stomach. His gut told him that The Max was the client. It sure as hell looked like the tip of the sliver goes right under the hotel. If it did, The Max, poor s.o.b., would have to slide it north a few feet. Probably cost a little more than the fifty thousand he wanted to pay for the piece. Whatta pain to move a forty story hotel, huh, Counselor Medford?

Addison Grant Medford III had been named after his grandfather, Addison Grant Medford I, a prominent Philadelphia doctor, and his father, Addison Grant Medford II, a Pennsylvania supreme court judge. The Grant was for Ulysses

S. Grant. Addison had taken considerable teasing about his name all his life. Being called the third was not uncommon in the private school or university he attended. It was being named after President U.S. Grant, maligned by history for an administration blanketed with a scandalous reputation for bribery.

Medford defended his namesake, reminding attackers of Grant's Civil War record, his brilliance as a tactician and his youth on attaining the presidency. At forty-six, Grant was the youngest ever to achieve such a status. Medford was only thirty-six. Who knows what he could achieve in ten years? There was time. Scandal would not touch him. He would be careful. Like his namesake, he would be a brilliant tactician. He would also have great power. Information was power. It was critical to have his sources well placed, and the best ones continued to be the ones he placed himself. The document that Murdock had provided from Franklin Trust was revealing. Coupled with information from his private detectives on the birth of a child made it explosive, offering new insights on how the matter might be handled. Trentino was due shortly. Medford's intercom rang as the door burst open. Little Vinnie Trentino never waited to be announced.

"You got good news, right? Last time it was all aggida." Trentino wore an open-necked black silk shirt under a black double breasted suit, a white silk handkerchief flapping out of the breast pocket and black wing tip shoes. He paced back and forth cracking his knuckles in rapid movements. Karlufsky, his bald dome offset by his walrus moustache, trailed behind his master's steps, towering over him, a great dane protecting an agitated cocker spaniel.

"Let's have it. When is Zeist closing?" demanded Trentino.

"Sit down, Vinnie, sit down. Relax a minute. Would you like a drink ? How about you, Karl?"

Trentino abruptly stopped pacing. Karlufsky almost bumped into him, but fortunately caught himself in time.

That would have been a serious breach of etiquette. Trentino bit his lip, shook his head and sat. He motioned to Karl to sit in the chair next to him. "You see, Karl, how nice he is to us. My expensive lawyer here. He is calming me down in advance, because he fucked up again. That's right counselor, ain't it? We got another problem. That's okay, I'm calm without the booze. Hey, you wanna drink Karl? You see, counselor, I want everyone to feel good before you hand out the bullshit. Okay, like I said before, let's have it."

Medford decided not to stand. He preferred having the desk between them. "Some new information has come to my attention. It appears the property does belong to a member of the Tyler family, as we had previously determined, but now there may be a question as to which one. Originally we were under the impression the sliver of land belonged to Margaret Tyler Crandall and were negotiating, through my stalking horse, to buy it from her. We were offering fifty thousand dollars."

"Listen, Medford, everybody knows I'm a reasonable man." Karl pursed his lips and nodded in confirmation. "You and Zeist wanna spend fifty. Twenty-five comes out of my pocket? I'm not gonna be no fly in your minestrone. Okay. Done." He clapped his hands and held his palms up to face the ceiling.

"Suppose she refuses and wants more?"

Trentino turned to Karlufsky and patted the giant on his arm. "I hope you're listening carefully, Karl. This is a lesson in negotiation. Listen, counselor, I ain't got the time for crapping around this week. Some very important people from Detroit are coming to see me. I may have to explain this whole story to them, so why don't you give me all the facts. And you better not leave nothing out. Not a fucking thing."

Medford rested his hand on the Tyler will synopsis. "It seems the Tyler woman had a child. The child might have an interest in the property."

"You didn't tell me there was a kid. How come you

didn't know about that ?"

"The reason I didn't advise you of this before is because, I wasn't sure until yesterday. Now, through some of my private sources, the fact has been confirmed. Seventeen years and eleven months ago, Margaret Tyler, unwed mother, gave birth to a seven pound four ounce infant girl. Father unknown. The child's given name is Sara."

"So buy it from the kid. Is that such a big friggin' deal?"

"No, it's not involved. It requires our buying a minor's interest. However, I have reviewed the survey and there is a distinct possibility that The Palace Hotel encroaches on the sliver of land in question. If this were indeed the state of fact, the asking price by this minor, or her advisor, might be considerably higher than fifty thousand dollars. It might be a million."

Trentino bolted upright. Medford smelled it. It was so tangible, he could feel it. Whenever there was a possibility of crisis, he could leap into the breach and control the scene. Others might panic, he would not.

"I spoke to Zeist and he told me to proceed. A substantially higher price than the fifty thousand is acceptable to him."

"Not with my money," Trentino said quietly.

Medford preferred that he shout. It was more of a known quantity. Trentino stood slowly, pulling himself to his minor height, rolled his shoulders and came to the edge of Medford's desk.

"This whole business better get straightened out in a hurry. I told you before. I got important people coming to see me this week. Do you remember the helicopter that crashed a few years ago with casino executives in it? If I think there is something you're holding back, there will be more than one body floating in Raritan Bay next week."

Medford felt his stomach twitch. What would U.S. Grant have done? The general was a risk-taker. Trentino also knows that information is power. The Tyler will synopsis was at his fingertips. Medford raised the document in the air.

"Is there something you want to show me?" asked Trentino. "Something special you want to tell me?"

"Yes."

Devlin sat on the edge of his bed, a damp towel on his freshly showered head. The only light in the room spilled past the half opened bathroom door. Ten-thirty. Not too late to call. He could have waited till morning and phoned her from his office, but this was better. He had the perfect excuse and wanted to hear her voice before they slept. His fingers found the numbers eagerly, like a puppy coming home. Oh, hell, what if her old man answers? Relax Devlin, you're all grown up now. It rang. He held his breath.

"Hello." It was her. Pure velvet.

"Mag, it's me." Silence. "It's Dev. Did I disturb you?"

"No, no, not at all. I was just sitting here alone, reading. I'm glad you called. I thought about our meeting and it was. . . .it was good to see you."

More silence. Why the hell couldn't he have waited until the morning and called from the office?

"Listen Mag, I went to the site where the piece of ground is and thought it best to call you tonight in case I missed you in the morning." That's better, that's better. Keep it business. He cleared his throat. Very official. "Seems to me The Palace Hotel might have encroached on your property."

"On my property," Maggie echoed. "If that's the case, fifty thousand is a very small price. I think an asking price of a million might be more in line with its value to solve their problem."

Devlin could barely control his urge to laugh aloud. This gal is all Tyler. Good old money-loving Tyler. "Good thinking, Maggie. Why not make it two million?"

"You're right," said Maggie. "Yes. That's the price. Two million."

Devlin was kidding and realized she wasn't. No question. All Tyler! She's probably got more nerve than old Jeremiah had. "Okay. You're the owner. I'll report your asking price. Shall I tell him there might be some room to negotiate?"

"Let's hear their response first. I'm glad you called me tonight. Now I can go to sleep with visions of sugar plums. Good night, Dev."

The phone clicked off. Devlin held it and visualized her face. What a combo. Steel and silk in one gorgeous package. But she's keeping her distance.

Maxwell Zeist knew the importance of support. Emotional as well as financial. He found his in a variety of sources, ranging from lawyers to Wall Street to beautiful young women. He also knew it was important to give support to others. Especially to those people who could help him. The people with the ability to pass new laws or, at times and more importantly, to change old laws. Election was only fifty days away. In addition to the contributions he made to Governor Charles Everett Radcliff's campaign funds, Zeist made it a point to have Radcliff as a frequent guest to his home in the Florida Keys. Radcliff also liked beautiful young women. And variety.

There were three of them. A redhead, a blonde and a jet black-haired Eurasian, all in brief bikinis. Tanya, the Eurasian, was smoothing sun tan lotion on Radcliff's back and legs, her small breasts spilling out of her even smaller bathing suit top. Zeist sat a table next to him, playing gin with the blonde. The redhead, topless, basked in the sun. Radcliff turned on his side to speak to Zeist and admire the redhead.

"The Attorney General's office sent me a copy of the prospectus for your new financing. When you complete it, you should have no problems with the Casino Commission on net worth. Have there been any questions about your borrowings from Brandywine Capital? You know, nothing was ever proven, but Trentino has been investigated twice."

Zeist folded the cards. "You win, Susie. Everett and I have some boring business to discuss, so why don't you girls go inside and leave the terrace to us." The trio quickly assembled their belongings and disappeared into the house.

"Sorry. You're right," said Radcliff.

"Again, for the record, I personally have never had any contact, or ever will, with Vinnie Trentino. By coincidence, he is represented, on his own behalf, by one of the law firms that also represents me. I know Brandywine Capital and Brandywine Services. I have been advised that they are legitimately organized corporations with whom my hotels should have no qualms doing business. Any investigation of Vinnie Trentino has nothing to do with me."

"My God, Max, what a speech. Did you think I had a tape recorder tucked under my jock strap? Why are you telling me this?"

Zeist smiled. "Everett, we're friends, so I feel comfortable sharing certain intimate facts with you." He lowered his voice. "This financing is absolutely vital to me. It's not just the Atlantic City hotels that are at stake. There is a minor title problem that could prevent a closing. My local attorney is negotiating the purchase of the property that is the source of the problem. I'm sure you understand without further explanations. I told you I'm not in any way partners with Trentino. It is, however, possible that we might have some community of interest. I believe one of his entities may receive, under certain highly specified conditions, a share of the Contingency Fund portion of the financing. In his anxiety for the event to take place, Little Vinnie, hot blooded Italian that he is, might do something inappropriate to hasten the event."

Radcliff wiped the suntan lotion off one leg with the

plush light blue terrycloth towel at his feet, flipping it over to the navy velour underside emblazoned with the silver MZ crest to wipe the other leg. He did it slowly and meticulously. "Max, I'm not one of your suckers at the slot machines. I'm nobody's fool and I'm nobody's errand boy. You just gave me this extended lecture of your distance from Vinnie Trentino and then I got the impression that you wanted me to call the NJ State Police to be sure nobody troubled Trentino while he was doing some of your dirty work. Sounds like obstruction of justice."

He stood and threw the towel on the chaise lounge. "My wife doesn't know about the women, but she does know I'm here."

"The players who enjoy my slot machines get paid off over eighty five percent of the gross. We are entitled to make a profit."

"Fine. The little people get a straight shake. Exactly what is it you're trying to tell me."

"It's simple. I may need your help, and you owe me."

Devlin had his breakfast at the diner at five-thirty. Evie Conroy had told him that Medford started his day at six. He couldn't sleep, anyway. Grace, his punctual bookkeeper, usually the first one in his office, would start the coffee, followed by Tess and finally Darlene, who spent the first fifteen minutes after her arrival in the bathroom putting the finishing touches on her makeup. He arrived well ahead of them today. Six-fifteen. He waited an hour and made his call.

The switchboard at Stern, Bradford and Altschuler was open twenty-four hours a day. Dev wondered if they billed for incoming calls on the same schedule. The automatic phone system informed him that Ms. Conroy wasn't in yet, but he could get anyone else's direct line by pressing the pound key and waiting for the directory. What the hell, it was only six-eighteen. Pressing M E D gave him Medford's number. Six, three, three. Remember never to play those at roulette.

"Medford."

I'll be so damned sweet and cheery, he'll get diabetes. "And good morning to you, Mr. Medford. This is R.J. Devlin."

"Yes."

"I met with Maggie Tyler – Ms. Crandall. You were right, she does need money and is happy to sell."

Medford smirked, reached toward the chess board and lay the black queen down in resignation. "Very good, very good. I can see you took my advice and convinced her of its nominal value. She must have been quite pleased to get a fifty thousand dollar offer."

"Well, not exactly, Mr. Medford."

"When you need money, you take what you can get."

Devlin had an almost uncontrollable urge to whistle. "I didn't say she was taking it. I said she was happy to sell."

"How much?"

This was going to be a pleasure. "Two million."

Medford's silence was an improvement over the classical music he had heard in the past month on this phone system. Poor Addison must have an upset stomach – and so early in the morning.

"When I said two million, I didn't mean she wanted that in addition to the fifty thousand you offered. She'll take an even two mill."

Medford reached for the black queen and set it upright. Not such a quick victory after all. "Apparently you didn't do such a good job convincing her it was worthless. I'll have to advise my client of this absurd price. Call me tomorrow."

Dev hung up the phone quickly. Man, it's hard to beat him to the punch on the abrupt hang-up. What thc hell, he's had years of practice. It's only six-thirty. It was a full day. Time to go home and take a nap. The ringing phone startled him. No nap.

"Good morning, South Jersey Title."

"Addison Medford. A question. Did Ms. Crandall ever have any children? If we have to buy a minor's interests, it might be an additional nuisance. Check it out."

Now it was Devlin's turn to feel his gut jump.

Chapter 5

TRENTINO'S parents lived in the same house in South Philadelphia where he had grown up. Those were his childhood roots. He visited there often, enjoying the accolades of neighbors who recognized his success. The one boy who had beaten him up and stolen his money when he was eight, now sold produce from a stand on Ninth Street near Catherine. Nobody had taken anything from Vinnie Trentino again.

The main offices of Brandywine Services and Brandywine Capital were in Fort Washington, near the Pennsylvania Turnpike. The location offered good access for his trucks, and himself, to the N.J. Turnpike, Interstate 295, the airport and the Atlantic City Expressway. Trentino always searched for a new road and always looked over his shoulder to see who was behind him. He spent half his waking hours in the car, often boasting of his two car phones. Even Carmine Dee, the capo di tutti capi, had only one.

Medford had all of Trentino's phone numbers. He waited until nine-thirty before informing Trentino of the new asking price. Let him enjoy his cappucino first. He'll be angry enough when he hears the amount. He could call Zeist later. If need be, Zeist would pay the two million. Little Vinnie Trentino never would.

It had been two hours since Medford questioned the existence of Margaret Crandall's child. Devlin controlled his apprehension until nine-thirty to seek an answer. He sat in his parked car on Decatur, around the corner from Maggie's. This time he would not hesitate to enter. He rang the bell. Maybe her old man will answer. Who gives a shit! Maggie opened the door.

"Dev! I wasn't expecting you." They stood there, trapped in the doorway, a lifetime since he had last entered it. A voice from the kitchen called out.

"Margaret, who's there?" Jonathan Crandall entered the foyer and stopped in his tracks at the sight of Devlin. He twisted the newspaper in his hand into a tight coil and threw it to the floor. "What are you doing here?"

"He came to see me, Father. It's business, about the piece of land."

Crandall picked up a small bag bearing the Atlantic City Country Club emblem. "I'm going to the club."

Devlin stepped aside as Crandall brushed past him. "In the future do your business over the phone. Don't ever come to this house again." Maggie and Devlin watched in silence as Crandall's green Lincoln Continental pulled away.

"Come into the kitchen, Dev. Would you like some coffee?"

"No, thanks. I'll stand right here, with one foot out the door, like always. Your father made it quite clear again that I'm still not welcome in this house."

"This is also my house. I'm a grown woman. No longer the little girl that has to obey her father. Come in."

He closed the door and took one step inside. She took his hand. "Maggie, before we go any further, I want to ask you about the abortion again. You put me off the other day." Her hand drifted from his. "You want to sell your land. You said you need the money. The lawyer told me there might be a child, and if there is, certain papers will have to be signed to buy a minor's interests. Do you have a child from your present marriage ?"

She shook her head. She retreated to the nearby wall. Her fingers clenched the thumb tucked inside a tightened fist.

"Well, Maggie? Is there something you want to tell me now?"

She shook her head again.

"Say it, dammit, say it! Admit it. Admit that we had a kid. Admit that you hid it from me. It's written all over your face. Damn you, spit it out! I want to hear you tell me."

"He hated you. My father hated you so much. He wanted me to get rid of the baby. But I couldn't do it. Dev, I couldn't, I couldn't," she sobbed.

She had lied to him. Always keeping him with one foot out the door. "Why couldn't you do it." He wanted her to suffer, the way he had. "What the hell was your problem? You're not even Catholic. Worried that the girls from Pilgrim Academy would find out Devlin got you pregnant?"

"Oh, Dev, can't you pity me? *I tell you I couldn't, couldn't, couldn't kill our baby."*

"Why didn't you tell me? Why am I always left out? Why do I always have to be on the outside looking in?"

"My father made me swear I would never tell you. I couldn't fight him then. The idea of my having your child drove him crazy. He only agreed to let me have the baby if we kept it a secret, especially from you. He swore he would never speak to me or my mother again if anyone ever found out that his grandchild had Devlin blood."

Devlin stepped back. The sting of rejection was deep and cruel. Did anyone approve of him? "What did your mother say?"

"My mother would do anything to calm down my father. And she wanted me to have the baby."

So he was a father. "Where is he?"

"It's not a he, it's a she. Sara."

Well, well. News for the Devlin clan. It appears he did bring his mother a grandchild after all.

"You remember, I left here in April. We told my friends that I was going on a vacation and then to check a few of the colleges where I had applied. My mother and I went to Palm Beach, to our house on Via Del Lago. Most of the neighbors leave in May. Nobody would see me with my. . . Sara was born on September ninth. There was a beautiful full moon over the ocean when our baby arrived."

"Where is she now?"

Maggie wiped the tears from her face and continued. "When we came back with Sara, my father said to keep her would only bring more shame to the family. We gave her to the Johnsons. Do you remember Trish and Alex Johnson? They used to be our gardeners."

Devlin shook his head in confusion. This was a mountain to digest. He had a daughter.

"Trish Johnson is a saint. And Alex is one of the sweetest men in the world. They're a Swedish couple about fifteen years older than us. They never had any kids and wanted so desperately to have a child. They begged and pleaded for Sara. I agreed if they would keep her close by and not move away until Sara went off to college. Trish thanked and blessed me to a point that I knew Sara was a gift from heaven."

Dev tapped himself. "Does she know. . . ?"

"No. She doesn't know about either of us, Dev. She doesn't know that you're her father, or that I'm her mother. There was never a formal adoption. She believes that her father died and her mother had to go away. They don't talk about it much. Her full name is Sara Maureen Johnson. The Maureen is after your mother. She feels Trish and Alex are her parents. They are wonderful to her, caring, loving and everything we would have wanted. They allowed my mother and me to make gifts to help out, to visit when she was little. Sometimes I see her now, from a distance. I never talk to her. Why should I disturb the life she has ?"

Devlin took Maggie's hand back into his. "You said she is close by. Where?"

"The Johnsons live in Linwood. Trish and Alex's best friends, Phyllis and Ed Matthews, live next door. The Matthews are the only ones, besides us, who know that I'm Sara's mother. Trish and Alex have no family. We had to tell someone close by in case of an emergency."

"Where in Linwood?"

"Berkley Court."

"Berkley Court! Maggie, that's just a few minutes from my office. She must go to Mainland High." Mainland High. His daughter strode the halls where he had been a hero. Did she ever hear the legend of the devil, Devlin? She was a Devlin. Did he ever pass her on the street? Probably did. His daughter.

"When can I see her?"

Maggie held Dev's face in her hands. "Can you forgive me, Dev?"

He shrugged. "Answer my question. When can I see her?"

"Soon."

Sara Johnson was one of the few students at Mainland High who was blessed with a car for her seventeenth birthday. She was deserving in many ways. Her maturity was well beyond her years, exhibited by her excellence in studies and an interest in business and accounting rarely found among other teenagers. She seldom brought anything but pleasure to Trish and Alex. Having the car was one of Sara's dreams fulfilled. A four cylinder LX Mustang Convertible. Red body, white interior and white top. The Mustang, the symbol of Mustang High, where she was a cheerleader. The dealer's asking price had been seventeen thousand, but he had come down to fifteen five. It wasn't too much of a financial hardship for Alex, between the money he had put aside and what Ellen Tyler Crandall insisted he take.

The car was free of debt, but Sara was responsible

for gas, maintenance and insurance. She managed those responsibilities by holding a part time job at Macy's in the Atlantic City Mall. Sara enjoyed the ride on the Black Horse Pike. Especially on the days when she could put the top down and feel her long blonde hair blow in the breeze. The sight of her in the red Mustang, her head shaking to the rock music beat, almost caused a few traffic jams.

Her job at the mall was simple. Stack the jeans, refold the sweatshirts left by most customers in a crumpled heap and occasionally handle the cash register. Ladies blouses were on a rack and needed periodic rearranging by size. That was her assignment today. She shifted row after row, switching the eights and tens out of the twelves and fourteens. As she lifted three bunched together a face suddenly appeared behind them. Sara started to smile, but the eyes stopped her. Flat grey eyes, startlingly devoid of expression. Her body chilled. She gasped and in the darkness of her momentary blink, the face disappeared. But the image would never leave her.

Zeist gently lifted the blonde's head from his lap, adjusted his trousers, and telephoned from his limousine. Never waste a moment. He had Medford's direct line and didn't have to deal with the annoying Stern, Bradford and Altschuler phone system. Medford answered.

"I got your message. What's the news on the land sliver, Addison?"

"Good news and bad news. The Tyler woman is ready to sell and we can wrap it up quickly."

"That's obviously the good news."

"She wants two million."

"That would cost me a million. What happened to the fifty or hundred thousand you were crowing about that your local stalking horse was going to produce?"

Medford loathed apologizing for someone else's failures. Did Devlin tell her to push up the price? No. Apparently not. Just a second rater that couldn't perform. "Max, it seems this Devlin, the local title man, fell flat on his face. The Tylers are used to having money and want more."

Zeist looked in the mirror and smoothed his hair. He looked incredible for fifty-two. At least ten years younger. "Did Radcliff call about anything?"

"No. Shall we negotiate the two million asking price?"

"Give it to them. If anybody complains, it's too bad. I won't jeopardize the bond financing. Call me when the papers are signed. I'll be in Manhattan. Goodbye, Addison."

Medford detested the idea of admitting to the second rater that he had resigned the field at the first confrontation; but he did not have to be humbled by making the call; Devlin was calling him.

"Yes."

"Good morning, Mr. Medford."

"That depends. You called."

What a turd this guy is. "I called to tell you that there is a child, so you will have to deal with buying her minor's interests."

Medford grudgingly gave an approving nod. The second rater found out about the child on his own. He said "her." He knows it's a girl. This new wrinkle didn't bother him, but Devlin did. What was it exactly about this man, probably his own age, that irritated him so much? What would be the best way to play him?

"Good, good. You're doing a fine job, Bob. By the way, you don't have to call me Mr. Medford, my friends call me Addison. And I've got good news on the price."

Devlin put his feet on the desk. Better keep them as high up as I can, the bullshit is stacking up in blizzard proportions. "That's great, Addison. She's going to be pleased with the two million. You know, what with a kid going to college and all."

"Yes, I thought that surely would please her, but I'm

afraid that we can't offer quite that much. Believe me, Bob, I prevailed on my client to do his best. I told him that Ms. Crandall had the heartbreaking misfortune of losing her mother recently and that she was getting divorced, but he felt that a million was more than a generous offer."

Dev lowered his feet off the desk. There was no safe place to escape the avalanche Medford was throwing. Devlin wished to hell he would stop calling him Bob. "She wants two."

"Whatever you say, Bob. Why don't I just prepare all the necessary documents and we'll see what we can work out. I'll prepare signature lines for Ms. Crandall and the child. Do you know her name?"

"Sara M. Johnson."

"Johnson? Not Tyler, Crandall, or Mattson, Ms. Tyler's husband's name?"

"It's Johnson."

"What is the M for?"

Dev swallowed before he could answer. "Maureen."

Berkley Court was a quiet, residential street off Shore Road. The neighborhood houses were middle class, built thirty and forty years ago but well maintained. Most of the homeowners were not summer shore visitors and worked locally. Trish and Alex Johnson lived in a three bedroom cape cod with one garage, at 59 Berkley. It was originally a two bedroom ranch. Alex had expanded the upstairs for the third bedroom when Sara turned twelve. It was a large room that covered half of the first floor of the house and gave Sara the privacy she wanted and the space to invite friends to sleep over. Phyllis and Ed Matthews lived next door at 61. Their daughter Jamie, four months older than Sara, was a frequent visitor at the Johnson house.

Grey Eyes sat in his black Buick, across from 59 and waited. He was used to waiting. He was used to new streets, unfamiliar cities. He came from a big city in the

Midwest, and had been all over the United States to do his job. To kill. Twenty-seven hits. Nothing ever traced to him. He was always careful. He had no mug sheet. He had no record. Not even a traffic ticket. There wasn't an official picture of him in any file in the country. Maybe the FBI had one. He had done women before, but this was the first time he had to do a kid.

It was Friday night. Her shift at the mall was over at nine-thirty. They told him she was a good kid, no drugs, no running with the wild ones. Saturday was another work day for her. She would be home before ten. Nine-fifty. A red Mustang LX, with the top down, was turning the corner onto Berkley. The other car was in the garage. Good. She'd have to park on the street, or the driveway.

He slunk in his seat and watched her pull into the driveway. Trish always left the lights on in the front till Sara came home. Grey Eyes scrutinized Sara's every move as she raised the white top of the Mustang and closed the windows. Her legs came out of the car first. The new light fixture that Alex had put on the house above the garage door gave excellent illumination. Let's see more of those legs. He rose three inches to get a better view.

She walked around the car with a chamois and wiped the side of the Mustang's shiny red body, rubbing the chrome runner, leaned over the hood, her breasts flattening on the metal, as she buffed its center in slow rhythmic strokes. Her skirt pulled up to reveal a firm shapely thigh. He licked his lips and grew hard. She stood away from the car, her long blonde hair swirling. Too bad. What a shame to waste her. He'd rather fuck her.

Chapter 6

TRISH was always the first one up and Saturday morning was no different. She worked a full week with Alex, handling two other landscape jobs in addition to the Tyler residence. The money was good, but abbreviated weekends remained the only time left to squeeze in the mountain of unfinished household duties. She was up a little earlier than usual, eager to get the apples for the apple cobbler that Sara loved. It was a recipe from the old country, given to her by Aunt Helga, and most delicious when the apples were freshly picked and juicy. Mike's Fruit and Produce in Egg Harbor had the best. Right off the farm. If she got there before the traffic to the shore started, she could pick out the cream of the crop.

Any extra effort was worth it to make her darling Sara smile. Sara, who brought such joy to them. She was a straight A student, loving, and reasonably obedient, only getting a little out of hand when her temper got the best of her. Where did she get *that* from? Neither Margaret nor any of the Tylers had much of a temper. Trish nudged her sleeping husband.

He rolled over to face her and peered through half opened eyes at the alarm clock. "Jeez, Trish, it's seven-fifteen. What the heck are you waking me up for? Tomorrow is church. This is the one day I can sleep an extra hour." He rolled over and buried himself under the covers. His muffled voice slipped out from under the pillow. "What are *you* up for at this hour? Sara doesn't go to work until eleven."

"Honey, please get up. I'm going to Mike's to buy apples."

"So go," he muttered.

"Alex, you have to drive me."

He threw the pillow off his head, blew air out of his mouth in exasperation and sat up. "Trish, you know how to drive. Why don't you just take the car out of the garage and go yourself?"

"I know you want to sleep late. So does Sara. Poor kid works hard and is exhausted. Her car is in the driveway. If we open the garage door, it will wake her up. You know I won't drive the Mustang. It's her baby and it makes me nervous, but she always lets you." Trish stroked Alex's face. "Come on, get up, you handsome Swede. You need a shave."

Alex rubbed his hands through his tousled dark blonde hair. It was only a shade deeper than Sara's and the similarity caused strangers to believe that the young beauty was really his. The idea always pleased him. What the heck, Sara likes the apple cobbler and so does he. Let the kid sleep.

Sara always left the keys to the Mustang in the blue ceramic bowl on the end table by the front door. The family key bowl. Alex fished them out. Trish left a note. "Honey – if you get up before we come back and you're looking for your car keys, don't worry. Nobody stole your red and white baby. We took it. Back soon. XXXX."

They quietly opened and shut the front door, settled into the red convertible, Trish fastened her seat belt and motioned for Alex to put on his. He adjusted the mirrors and started the car down the driveway. The explosion was deafening.

The first blast scattered parts of the car half a block

away. One wheel hit the Matthews' house next door, smashing the front window. Sections of mangled red auto body spewed on the lawn, reflecting the searing flames blazing on the remaining chassis. The reeking acid smell of burnt flesh mixed with the odor of gasoline. Flaming red fingers leaped up, licking the side of the house below Sara's window. The second eruption flipped over the devastated frame like a toy.

Within minutes startled neighbors appeared to explore the source of the booming sounds. Ed Matthews rushed from his kitchen to see his shattered window and peered out to the street. He saw the flames in the driveway next door and shouted for his wife and daughter.

Sara had bolted upright in her bed. Her room was in the front of the house over the garage, facing the street. She called for Trish. No answer. She looked out the window and saw her cherished car in flames. Oh, no! Who did this? What crazy jealous kids did this? She raced down the stair, her face flushed with anger and despair. Maybe it wasn't her car. She looked for the keys in the blue bowl. She saw the note. Trish and Alex had taken her car. What was that in the driveway? She opened the front door. Scorching heat attacked her, stinging her skin, searing her eyes. She turned her head and saw it on the lawn. The license plate. SARA 17. She forced her eyes open and looked at the burning wreck again. *OH, NO, NO, NO, NO, NO!* She flew down the four steps onto the front lawn. The flames drove her back. Trish's purse, undamaged, lay there next to the license plate. Sara ran around the car praying for some miracle. Tears streamed down her face. She scratched at her arms and screamed again and again.

"TRISH, TRISH, PLEASE, SOMEONE HELP ME. ALEX. OH, PLEASE, SOMEONE HELP, HELP, HELP. SAVE THEM. OH, MOMMY."

Ed and Phyllis Matthews ran to her, followed by Jamie. Phyllis covered Sara with a robe and pulled her away from the inferno toward the Matthews' house. Sara broke free and screamed again.

"No, don't leave them here. Mr. Matthews, please, please help me save them."

Sara's arms flailed in the air. Ed Matthews held her with both his arms and dragged the frantic girl through his front door. A tearful Jamie followed, stroking Sara's hand. A neighbor stepped forward to help. Matthews waved him away, shouting, "Call the police!"

Officer Valerie Yankovitch was on the board and took the call. Radio dispatch had it within thirty seconds. The local TV and radio stations with scanners picked it up without delay. WACTV was the first to televise it. A car bombing in a quiet residential neighborhood. That was news that deserved an immediate release. But, it was still local. Network news came first and they wouldn't break the full local story until the eight to nine segment. At eight-o-nine, the flash bulletin appeared on the bottom of the screen during a commercial. Details would follow.

Maggie was finishing her morning exercise regimen. She stopped the treadmill, stood riveted to the TV screen and cursed Chet Blakely, the morning anchorman, for the delay. In forty-five seconds that seemed an eternity, he returned to announce the known current information.

"Alex and Trish Johnson, of 59 Berkley Court, Linwood, were killed this morning when their red 1993 Mustang convertible exploded at approximately seven-thirty. No other parties reported injured. Mr. Johnson was a local landscaper. The police have made no comments on the cause of the explosion. We will bring you full details of this tragedy on the five o'clock news. Sports and the weather. . . ." Maggie clicked it off.

She sat on the bed. Her heart raced and her skin was clammy. Calm. Calm. Be calm. Control yourself. Now is no time to lose your head. She dialed the Johnson's number. Ten, twelve, thirteen rings. No one answered. The Matthews. She didn't have their number. Dammit. Why isn't it in my book? The only reason they knew her secret was in case of an emergency. She dialed information.

"Matthews, on Berkley Court, Linwood. And please hurry, it's an emergency."

Maggie rocked and prayed as she sat on the edge of the bed, waiting in agony for the phone number. A sing-song voice responded. "There is an Edward Matthews and also a phone for listed for Jamie Matthews, both at 61 Berkley Court in Linwood."

"Yes, yes, that's the one. Edward."

A recording followed with the number and the offer of dialing it for a charge of thirty-five cents. Maggie's trembling fingers raced and made the call. Phyllis answered.

"Phyllis, it's Maggie. I just heard it on the news."

"We expected your call. It was horrible beyond words. I don't think they suffered. It was over in seconds. The police said it wasn't an accident. It was a bomb. Don't ask me questions, I don't have any answers. Poor Trish and Alex were the sweetest people in the world. They didn't have enemies. Everybody loved them. What kind of an animal would do a thing like this? "

"Where is Sara?"

"She's upstairs in Jamie's room, sobbing her heart out. She doesn't understand what happened. Poor darling is lost. We're all so confused. Who would want to hurt them? It's probably some kind of grotesque, horrible mistake and Trish and Alex were the victims of it."

Maggie paced as she listened. Maybe it's not a mistake. Maybe the event was planned, but the wrong victims were killed. The thought is bizarre, but maybe it was Sara there were after. But why? "Phyllis, you and Ed have been wonderful. I thank you for Sara. For my daughter. I'll be over there as soon as I can. It's time she knew the truth."

"That's for you to decide. We'll talk about it when you get here."

"There is someone else who also will be there. You don't know him, but you'll meet him today. He's very much a part of everything. He happens to live close by. Right there in Linwood. I'll see you as soon as I can. Goodbye,

Phyllis."

Maggie took her wallet from her purse and removed Dev's business card from its hidden location. Why did she tuck it behind her driver's license? Afraid her father would see it? Dev's home number was on the card. He answered abruptly.

"Dev, it's me. Maggie."

"I'm just running out the door. My Saturday morning basketball game. What's up ?"

"You obviously haven't heard the news."

"What's the matter, you sound terrible. Is it your father?"

"No. Trish and Alex were killed."

Dev felt his heart fall and his adrenaline pump. His daughter. "Sara, anything happen to her ?"

"They were driving her car, but she wasn't in it."

"That's terrible. Where did it happen ?"

Maggie hesitated telling him all the facts. Information that would soon hit the national news. She was still afraid of his temper. "It happened in their driveway. Apparently a car bomb, not an accident. I don't know anything else, so please don't ask me any questions. I'm going there right now. It's heartbreaking to have to meet her this way, at a time like this. I called because I knew you would want to be there too."

"I'll be there, probably before you will."

Maggie quickly asserted, "Don't go in before I get there!"

"I won't. I'll wait in front of the house, in the car."

"It's 59. No, 61, next door. Do you know where it is?"

"Yeh. I've already driven by it."

It was only a five minute drive, but Devlin drove at a snail's pace. If he arrived too soon before Maggie, he wasn't sure he could stop himself from bounding up the stairs into the house to his daughter's side. As he approached the scene, he could see the fire department extinguishing the embers of the car and the small flames on the Johnson house. The morning air remained heavy with the smell of burning gasoline and smoke. Gawking neighbors, some dressed in bathrobes or pajamas, attracted to the spectacle were pushed back by the firemen. Two uniformed policemen and someone in plain clothes were talking to the Matthews. Devlin stopped half a block away, watched and waited.

Maggie's car pulled up next to his. They got out, heads down, with the drawn faces of worried parents. They embraced, held hands and walked slowly to the Matthews. The police stopped the interrogation and faced them. Maggie, Phyllis and Ed put their arms around one another, huddled in a circle, hugging, crying and bemoaning the loss of Trish and Alex. The large heavyset man in plain clothes waited for their moment of grief to subside.

"Excuse me, ma'am, I'm Detective Haines. You are...?"

"Crandall. Margaret Crandall. And this is Robert Devlin."

Phyllis put her arm on Maggie's shoulder. "She's a friend of the family."

Maggie nodded to Devlin, and quickly added, "So is he."

"Do you know anything about this bombing that might be helpful in the investigation?" Haines asked.

Devlin and Maggie exchanged glances. Maggie shook her head. Haines turned to Devlin. "And you?"

"No." Devlin would get his own answers.

Detective Haines handed each his card. "Call me if you think of anything that might be of interest to the police." He motioned to the uniformed men and they left.

The four stood in silence, unsure of their next course of action. Maggie spoke first. "Phyllis, this is the man that I mentioned to you on the phone."

Phyllis turned to Dev, smiled and, with inquisitive eyes, stared back at Maggie. Maggie nodded. This was the father. Devlin endured the examination and noted that Ed did not offer his hand. Ed led them into the house and they sat in the living room, waiting for Sara's appearance.

"Maggie, maybe you should wait a few days before you say anything. At least until after the funeral. The poor child is so confused already. She shouldn't be burdened further."

They heard voices at the top of the stairs. Jamie came down with Sara trailing slowly behind her. "Mom, I gave Sara some aspirin and she's still got a bad headache. What else have we got?"

The two girls stopped at the sight of Maggie and Dev. Jamie stared at Devlin, a glint of recognition in her eyes. Maggie jumped to her feet, and warily approached Sara. Phyllis put her hand on Maggie's arm.

"Girls, this is Maggie Crandall and Robert Devlin. They were both good friends of Trish and Alex and wanted to pay their respects."

Jamie whispered into Sara's ear. "That's Devlin. You know. From Mainland High. His pictures are in the hallway near the gym entrance."

Sara had eyes only for Maggie. She came closer, her tear-stained face almost touching Maggie's.

"Who are you?" asked Sara in a small weary voice. "Wait, wait, I know you. I remember, you're the pretty lady that used to come to visit when I was little. Then you stopped coming, but I thought I'd see you sometime. When I was about ten or eleven, you'd be watching me. But you never came over to talk to me. Who are you?"

Maggie longed to take her in her arms. So close. "I'm. . . .I'm your mother."

Sara leaped away from the face, from the words. "No! No! No! No! You're not my mother. Trish said my mother loved me, but she had to go away when I was little – but she would come back. You were here, you saw me. If you were my mother you wouldn't have stayed away. You would have talked to me."

Tears streamed down Sara's cheeks. She slapped

them, frantically seeking reality. "Trish and Alex are dead--who is going to take care of me?"

Devlin stepped towards the heart broken girl. "She really is your mother. Don't worry, Sara, we'll take care of you."

Sara glared at him. "We? What do you mean, we? Who are you ? What are you – her damn boyfriend?"

"No. . . .I'm your father."

Sara gasped, looked to heaven, and started to fall as Devlin caught his daughter in his arms.

Chapter 7

DEVLIN rarely suffered a bad night's sleep since he was twelve. Lately, he rarely had a good one. That was only one of the things that changed. This week had been one of the worst in his life. He and Maggie talked on the phone till after twelve every night. There was one good turn that came out of the nightmare. They were communicating, reminiscing, getting closer. They had a common cause.

Trish and Alex had been active members of good standing in their Lutheran church and Pastor Gruntdveig arranged the funeral. Visitors were sparse during the three-day mourning period, a few neighbors, two of Alex's old customers and a dozen of Sara's school friends. Devlin and Maggie were there every day but kept a respectful distance, allowing Sara breathing room, understanding her continuing resentment of them both.

Jamie was a constant, warm, supportive source of comfort for Sara, along with the other girls who surrounded her. They all took their turns staring at Devlin. Whispers of, "He's gorgeous! He is so hot," were often followed by girlish giggles that lightened the day. They reminded Sara that her father was the greatest athlete in the history of Mainland High. He was the "legendary Devlin."

One afternoon, Sara stood next to him, allowing his arm on her shoulder, enjoying the envious glances of her school mates. Once she brought him coffee. Maggie wasn't sure where she fit in, watching her teenage daughter slowly getting a crush on her new-found father, yet still silently reproaching her.

Dev returned to Maggie and they observed Sara. Hopefully, the idea of her being their daughter was sinking in and becoming more acceptable to her. They knew they had a good ally in Jamie. By the end of the week, Sara no longer frowned when she saw them. But she rarely smiled. Flashes of resentment toward Maggie were a daily occurrence. Mutterings to Jamie, of, "Where was she all those years ? I would never abandon my child," were purposefully audible and pierced Maggie's heart. It would take more time to heal and many explanations were still to be made. Sara was a member of their little clan and entitled to know the history.

Devlin's meeting with Frank Holenka was another matter that ruined his sleep. It brought periodic nightmares. Holenka was captain of detectives of the Atlantic City police. He was also someone Dev had known all his life. The Holenka family had lived two houses away from the Devlins and Frank was big brother Danny's best friend. Kid brother, Bobby Devlin, three years their junior, was ever at their heels in worshipful eagerness to be included. Lucky for him he was not. During their teenage years, Frank and Danny ran with Jimmy Bonifante.

When he was twenty-three, Jimmy Bonifante ended up in the state penitentiary, convicted of armed robbery. At seventeen he stole a car. He also stole his father's gun and put it in the glove compartment. It was a clear summer night, Jimmy decided to go for a joy ride. Nobody knew the car was hot. Why not have some company? Frankie and Danny were always good for laughs. He had extra moola in his kick; he would stake them all to beers.

The three wound up at Randy's Ribs & Ale, the

road house on the Pike. At two in the morning, with beer and scotch mixed in his belly, Jimmy took the wheel. The truck he crashed into ten minutes later was on its way to Jersey City with a load of produce. The truck driver veered to avoid the collision, but the six wheeler wound up against a telephone pole. The three boys lay sprawled in the car, jolted, but conscious. Frankie was stretched out on the back seat. His head dangled to the floor.

The driver was shaken but not injured. The truck driver's helper was dead on impact. The driver wiped the blood from the face of his friend, reeled out of the truck, and staggered to the battered car. He pulled open the car door, and tore at Jimmy's shirt.

"You dumb son-of-a-bitch. You killed Eddie! I'd like to kill you with my own hands. When the troopers come, I'm gonna tell them how you ran us off the road."

He pushed himself into the car, grabbed Jimmy by the hair with one hand, by the throat with the other. "I can smell your stinkin' breath, you drunken piece of shit!"

He squeezed harder at Jimmy's neck. Jimmy gasped for air, his eyes rolled upwards. Danny struck at the driver's arms and hands but couldn't budge their grip. With a surge of strength, Jimmy broke free of the vice-like hold and pulled the gun from the glove compartment. He would kill this bastard. Danny's reaction was immediate. He smashed the gun from Jimmy's hand.

When the case came to trial, Jimmy testified that neither Frankie nor Danny knew anything about the stolen car or the gun. Jimmy received his first prison sentence. Frankie and Danny were on probation and ordered to do two years of community service. The fates had sent the two friends down paths that changed their lives in positive ways. Danny's was to the seminary and priesthood. Frankie Holenka became a police officer. Danny also extracted a promise from his younger brother.

Dev saw Holenka frequently over the years, usually around one of the casinos or the Shamrock Pub for beer and darts. It was never official, except for the time Dev had knocked out a tourist's two front teeth. The tourist, a six-foot four auto dealer from Baltimore, decided he wanted Dev's date of the evening for his own. The tourist told the little local boy to take a walk and pushed Devlin a bit too hard to send him on his way. Frank was Dev's character witness that helped dismiss the charges.

Today's meeting, sitting in Frank's car, was different. Dev had asked Holenka, a guy with muscle on the Atlantic City force, to follow up the Linwood police. Holenka took off his silver rimmed sunglasses and focused his steel blue eyes on Devlin.

"Okay, hot shot title ace, what's your involvement with this ruckus?"

"Because, like you said, I'm a title hot shot. Major league Philly law firm needs someone to find out who owns a piece of land. Very complicated, but they recognize talent so, of course, they hired me." Devlin grinned and stroked his hair.

"Right. I can see you're still keeping your press clippings. So then?"

"Alright, alright. It seems the piece of land is owned by an old friend of mine. Maggie Crandall. The Johnsons, the couple that got killed, I never knew them before, were her gardeners for many years."

"Hey, Bobby, come on. Nobody kills someone because they forgot to pull the weeds or water the rosebush."

"Wait, wait, Frank. There's a lot more I haven't filled you in on. The piece of land in question is a small sliver that lies between Balley and The Palace. If my calculations are correct, it's actually under The Palace, which you know is owned by The Max. I got a suspicion that Mr. Maxwell Zeist is the client behind the Philadelphia lawyer, who, incidentally, is a class A pain in the ass."

Holenka took a memo book out of the glove compartment and wrote, "Zeist and Attorney General."

"I heard something last week about The Max that I

want to check out. If you think Zeist is behind this, my bet is you're off base. It's not his style. Zeist might rub a shoulder or two with a few wrong apples, but his main buddies are the creme de la creme. He wouldn't want any bad p.r. that might get to the ears of the rich and famous and ruin his golden image."

Devlin drummed his fingers on the window. "Do you have any clues on the bombing that are worth anything?"

"Nothing to write home about. The lab reports aren't finished. Something might show up there, but I doubt it. The guy who did it was a pro. I don't understand all your title mumbo jumbo, or why they would want to kill anyone involved with that sliver of land, but if it makes you feel any better and it helps you with your client, I'll tell the local boys to watch the house. Police protection might not be the right answer. If it is Zeist, and I told you I doubt it, he's very thick with Governor Radcliffe. Radcliffe is ass- hole buddies with the state police."

Devlin clenched his fist and banged on the dashboard. "If any son-of-a-bitch tries it again, I'll kill them."

Holenka put his sunglasses back on and faced Devlin.

"Don't talk stupid, Bobby. I'll give you three reasons why you couldn't kill anyone." He reached into his shirt pocket and pulled out a pack of gum. He put two sticks in his mouth and offered the pack to Devlin. "First, because it's against the law, and with all your wild talk, you're basically law abiding. Afraid your mom will come down from heaven and make you do a few Hail Marys. Second, I don't think you got the nerve to pull a trigger or slit a throat. And third, and for sure the heaviest in my book, is the promise you made to Danny. Remember, kid, it's your mortal soul."

Devlin bit his lip, and ran his fingers through his hair again and again. "Son of a bitch better stay away from her."

Holenka, from behind his dark sunglasses, examined

Devlin's face closely. He could see the tears at the corner of the eyes. He hadn't seen Bobby cry since he was nine. The time he and Danny had smacked the pesty kid brother because he followed them to the movies. Holenka patted Bobby Devlin's shoulder gently.

"What are we having this conversation for? By your own admission, you didn't even know Alex and Trish Johnson. What are you so uptight about? Be sensible, Bobby, who were they to you? The car that was bombed wasn't even theirs. It's registered to Sara M. Johnson."

Devlin shaded his eyes with a cupped hand. "Yeh, I know. The M is for Maureen."

"So?"

"She's my daughter."

Grey Eyes made his calls to clients from a public phone. He preferred ones on a busy street in a bad neighborhood. He spoke into the mouthpiece in a flat monotone that matched his eyes.

"You seen the stuff on TV. I don't like it when the wrong party gets it. You gave me bad info. You said the kid is the only one that used the Mustang. This makes me look bad."

The only response was a grunt. Grey Eyes understood. It was still up to him. "Next time she goes and it's hands on."

Whenever there was a difficult question to answer in the office, the girls came to Devlin. When he had a problem, he sought out Tess or Jake. Devlin had struggled with the riddle by himself and turned to Tess. Alex and Trish had no enemies, owed no money of consequence and were faithful to one another. They quickly concluded that Sara was the intended victim. Sara was the potential heiress to a fortune. But what good would killing her do? Who could possibly benefit from her death? Who knew she was Maggie's daughter, or had Tyler blood? The one person that seemed a candidate with some of the answers was Medford. But that was a source of information they knew would be closed. The question plagued them. Why would anyone want Sara dead? They sat in baffled silence. Devlin drew faces on the styrofoam cup, emptied of the good diner coffee. Tess stroked her round belly.

"By the time we figure this one out, my kid will be ten. I give up, Dev. Let's call Jake. He always comes up with something."

Devlin nodded, stabbed the face on the styrofoam cup in the forehead with his BIC pen and hit Jake's automatic dialing button. They waited for his voice on the speaker.

"Good morning. Jake Balaban."

"Jake, good morning. It's Dev, Tess and the baby. Did you think about the problem we talked about?"

"Good morning. Tess, how are you feeling? How come that slave driver doesn't give you some maternity leave?"

"I'd go nuts in the house, Jake. Besides I charge him minimum wage for junior."

Jake's grandfather had been a union organizer for the AFL and approved of Tess and her humor. "I'll tell you both. The answer, to my way of thinking, is a simple one provided you have the right information."

"Provided we have the right information," Devlin echoed. "Very good, Jake. Between you and Tess, I'm surrounded by comedians."

Jake responded quickly. "No, no, no, no. I'm serious. This is a puzzle and you don't have all the pieces. You should know, Mr. Devlin, that we are in a business of information and it usually comes in the form of a document. You are missing a document. And I wouldn't be surprised if it's recorded somewhere."

Tess and Devlin smiled at one another. Devlin raised the punctured styrofoam cup in a mock toast. "Okay, Jake," he said, " but what if it's *not* recorded. Where do we find it?

Whose desk or mattress do we ransack?"

"It seems to me, your Philadelphia lawyer should be the first place to try."

Tess leaned sideways toward the speaker, her stomach preventing a forward move. "Jake, the idea of a missing document is good, but we already concluded we wouldn't get diddly out of Medford."

"That tight ass s.o.b." Dev turned to Tess bowing his head in apology, "Pardon, little mother, he wouldn't give directions to a blind man trying to cross the railroad tracks."

Tess snapped her fingers. "Evie! Maybe she'll tip us if there is a key document that he's got."

"Good," said Jake. "I don't know who Evie is, but if Tess thinks it will work and if you can get all the documents on the matter, you should have your answer."

"Listen, Jake, in Tess's enthusiasm, she forgot to tell you that Evie is Medford's secretary. She may not be so hot about the idea of rifling her boss's files. But just suppose she would extend a small favor to us, what should we ask for? Documents come in all sizes, shapes and subjects. We can't ask her for the entire filing cabinet."

Both Devlin and Tess leaned toward the phone, waiting for Jake's response. No voice came from the speaker. They shouted as one. "Jake, are you there?"

"I'm thinking, I'm thinking. It seems to me, if you've got a single shot, and can ask for only one document, I'd ask for one that probably was never recorded."

Dev tried to think like Jake would but concluded he couldn't. "Like what?" he asked.

"A will."

Chapter 8

DEVLIN arrived at his office at nine and decided not to call Evie first thing. It was Monday morning. She was bound to be busy and would not appreciate starting her day with a request to surreptitiously pull files from Stern, Bradford and Altschuler. It was a heavyweight favor to ask. It wouldn't be unreasonable if she just said, no. But, as the guys on Dev's basketball team always said, if you don't ask, you never get laid. Dev and Tess decided to wait until after lunch.

The diner was jammed with truck drivers and tourists. Nick gave them Dev's regular corner booth, told them to get the moussaka and raced back to the kitchen at the sound of crashing crockery. Tess had one poached egg and cup of tea. Dev had a medium Greek salad, the pea soup and the moussaka. He was edgy over the day's activity so he skipped dessert.

They were back at the office at one-fifteen and called Evie on Dev's speaker phone. After the opening trauma of the automatic phone system and no answer on Evie's direct line, they pressed O for the operator. The operator informed Tess that Ms. Conroy was not in and was taking a leave of absence. Tess hung up and they stared at one another grimly.

"That's pretty sudden. Tess, this smells to high heaven. Have you got Evie's home phone number?"

"No. She moved about two months ago. Maybe I've got it home. Wait, wait, she moved to Wyncotte. Her husband's name is David. Let me try information. That's 215, right?"

Devlin nodded, Tess tried to lean forward to dial, but was impeded by her stomach. Devlin picked up the phone. "You look like the Goodyear blimp coming in for a landing. I'll get it."

The number was listed in Wyncotte. He dialed on the speaker phone. Three rings and a voice was speaking to them. "You have reached the Conroys. David and Evie are out right now – – hello, hello. Wait till I turn this off."

Tess and Dev high fived each other.

"Evie, this is Dev. Tess is with me. What the hell are you doing home at one-thirty on a Monday afternoon. You retired?"

"Yeh, I certainly am. Thanks to you. I've been fired."

"Thanks to me? What are you talking about?"

"I'm terribly sorry, Evie," said Tess. "I know you just bought the house. What a lousy time to lose your job. What did you mean about Dev? Is that a joke?"

"No, it's not a joke. At least to me it isn't. David is furious. He's talking about suing the law firm, Medford personally. Hey, am I on a speaker? Is anyone else in the room?"

Dev and Tess looked at each other in amazement.

"Yes, Evie, you are on the speaker, and there is no one in the room but Tess and me. What the hell is going on?"

"I'll tell you what the hell is going on, in chapter and verse. A little over a month ago I called up Tess to get you some title work. You were hired to buy a piece of land for fifty thousand dollars. Within a few short weeks you come back to Medford and tell him the asking price is two million. Dev, I knew damn well that Maggie, or her family, owned the piece of land. I told Medford you knew her. There was nothing wrong with that. Now he thinks I gave you some information and that's why the price went up. He called me a Judas for helping that third rater Devlin. Then he fired me. Before my year end bonus. David and I were depending on that money for the house."

"Hey, hey, whattya mean third-rater? He treated me like a second rater. My rating must have gone down when Maggie's price went up."

"Yeh, very funny, very funny. You're laughing and I'm out of a job. Medford was a taskmaster, but the pay was great."

"Evie, I have a major favor to ask. I swear to you, I would never ask it, if it weren't so important."

"This better be simple."

Dev felt the sweat between his shoulder blades. His voice was hushed and husky as he leaned on the desk, his mouth almost touching the speaker.

"I think there are documents Medford has that have a material effect on the value of this sliver of ground. Or if not the value, something to do with its ownership. There is a key piece to this jigsaw puzzle that I don't know about."

Evie laughed. "You bet there is, Mr. Rocket Scientist. You certainly are missing something. It's called a will."

Dev sat upright and pointed to the circled word, WILL, on the yellow legal pad and shoved it to Tess. Jake was on the money again.

"I've got to see it, Evie. It's a matter of life and death. Get me a copy. Please."

"You're incredible. You never were bashful, but this is unbelievable. I've just been fired from a job that I desperately needed because my employer thought I was feeding you information, which I wasn't. And now you want me to go back to the same office and get some private papers for you. If I could, I wouldn't, and anyway, I can't."

"Why can't you ?"

"Because the original is in the vault of the Franklin Bank and Trust Company."

Devlin pounded the desk. Tess turned thumbs down.

"Shit, that place is Fort Knox."

Evie was enjoying this. The great Devlin couldn't get his way. Let him suffer, the way she was. Now she could rub a little salt in the wounds. "No, you can't get into Franklin Trust, but there's a copy in my computer in the office."

Tess and Devlin shouted together in triumph. "Great!" sang Dev, "Get me a printout!"

"You don't listen. I said before, if I could, I wouldn't and I can't anyway. And the reason I can't is, because the s.o.b. fired me and I am no longer allowed access to the files."

Dev and Tess were silent as Evie looked around her half finished kitchen wondering how she was going to pay the tile man. She turned back to the phone. "I don't know why you have to see this will, Dev, but please don't tell me it's a matter of life and death. What it really is, is simply a matter of money. Believe me, we all have our money problems. You and Maggie will manage just fine. Probably a lot better then David and I will. Goodbye, Tess."

Dev lunged at the speaker. "Evie, wait, please, please, don't hang up yet."

"What?"

"This *is* about life and death. Did you read about the car bombing in Linwood ? Two people, a man and a woman were killed."

"David and I saw it on TV."

Dev looked at Tess while he continued the conversation. He could always tell Tess anything. "Evie, I'm asking you to help me get some information. Maybe I should give you some in exchange. The couple that were killed, Trish and Alex Johnson, were the surrogate parents to a beautiful seventeen-year-old girl named Sara. If you saw Sara, especially if you saw her down at the South Carolina and Tennessee beach, with her long blonde hair flowing in the wind, she'd rattle your memory. Lord knows, she did mine. Do you know who her real parents are?"

Tess held her stomach and moaned. "Oh, Dev."

Evie listened to the clock tick on kitchen wall. The beach at Tennessee, a lifetime ago. "Yes, I think I do."

"She belongs to me and Maggie. Now that I've found her, I'm not letting her go. We're going to be a family. For some reason that I don't understand, Medford, or Zeist, or someone tried to kill her, and killed two innocent people instead. Evie, you've got to help us. Maybe the will can shed some light on it." He swallowed hard, fighting his tears. "Please, Evie, please, I'm begging you."

Evie Conroy tried to stand and could not. She had started this entire chain of events. She had convinced Medford to call Devlin. She had known about Maggie. Two people were dead. Was Medford capable of these acts? Vinnie Trentino was. Everybody was motivated by money. Even her. For her year end bonus.

"There may be a way for you to get a copy of the will. But I don't want to answer you now. Let me talk to David. Let me sleep on it. . . ."

"Evie, the time is vital."

"I know. I promise you an answer in the morning."

Devlin had another night of tossing and turning. At seven-forty he was sitting on the edge of his bed trying to pick up his left shoe with the big toe of his right foot when the phone rang. He was sure it was Maggie and for the first time he hoped it would be someone else. He hoped it would be Evie. It was Tess.

"Wake up, you sleepy head."

"I'm up, I'm up."

"Evie called me a half an hour ago and said she can't get a copy of the will because she won't go to the office."

"A half an hour ago! Why didn't you call me?"

"Listen, Bobby Devlin, when you get to be in my condition, you will also take care of nature's calls before business calls. Anyway, last night she had a long talk with her husband. David said that Medford is cold hearted enough to commit murder and is probably behind the whole scheme and should be hung by his balls. Evie disagreed with the first part of statement, but agrees with the hanging. She thinks someone else did the bombing. Now for the eight o'clock morning good news. She hopes the rat gets caught and has agreed to help."

Dev stood on the top of his bed, shifting his weight back and forth, using the mattress for a trampoline. This whole bit may be fun. "How is she going to help if she won't go back to the office?"

"She wants *you* to go to her office, or as she said, her old office. Tonight. Get there between eleven and midnight. She wants to check a few things first and will call us at four this afternoon with all the details on how you are going to do it."

Dev jumped higher, trying to touch the ceiling, warming up for the race.

"Devlin, what the hell is that noise? Are you listening to me?"

He plopped to a sitting position. "Heard every word you said. I'll see you in the office. Tell Grace to warm up her mud coffee, I can handle anything today."

Dev showered and checked his beard in the mirror as he dried himself off. The damn dark stubble grew too fast, especially in the summer. Gotta look clean and spiffy. Especially for the morning stop on Berkley. When she hugged me yesterday, it was tough to let her go. Those eyes of hers are like Maggie's. The blue of the sky. But I think the lass has the Devlin temper.

Time to check on all his girls. He called Maggie, told her what progress was being made with Evie and promised to speak to her before the trip to Philly. Next call was to Sara. Jamie answered the phone. They both were staying home from school for the rest of the week.

"Sara is still asleep, Dev. I mean Mr. Devlin."

"It's okay, Jamie, you can call me Dev. Don't wake

up Sara, just tell her I called and you can kiss her for me."

"I will, Dev." Oh, God, I wish he'd kiss me. I'd die with a smile on my face. "Coming over later?"

"I'll try. Bye, honey."

Jamie took a deep breath and repeated "honey" aloud. She hummed as she walked outside to get the morning paper. The police car circled again and the uniformed arm waved to her. A black car was at the corner. Flat grey eyes stared at her from a distance.

The day dragged by for Tess and Devlin as they watched the clock tick off its sluggish advance to four. Dev wanted to shoot over to see Sara, but was afraid Evie might call and he would miss her. She called at three fifty-seven. Her promise was solid, Devlin hoped her plan was, too. He and Tess went into his office and put the call on the speaker.

"Okay, here's the way we're going to do it. Today is Thursday and I was right about the hour. Devlin, arrive at the building between eleven-thirty and twelve. There are always word processors working late to pump out contracts that have to be reviewed the next day. Some juniors are burning the midnight oil, pushing to make partner, and they also will be floating around. What with people going to the bathroom, and the cleaning staff going from room to room, you shouldn't be noticed in all the commotion. At one hundred seventy-five an hour for a junior and three-fifty for a partner, Stern, Bradford is thrilled to see late night activity and keep up the billing. They'd love to do it twenty-four hours a day. You know where the building is?"

"Yeh. The Packard Building at Fifteenth and Chestnut."

"Right. At the hour you're coming, cross the Ben Franklin Bridge to Center City and pick up the Vine Street Expressway. Park at the garage across from the building. Wear a suit, a tie and carry a briefcase."

"You've already given him a problem," said Tess.

"Come on, guys, this is serious. Listen closely, Dev. I've drawn a map of the office and David will fax it to you before six. Stern, Bradford has the seventh and eighth floor. My office is on the eighth. I drew a circle around Medford's office and put an M on it. My desk is just to the left of his door. Dev, do you know Word Perfect ?"

He nodded. "Yes, he knows it. Answer her, you idiot!" shouted Tess.

"My computer is hooked up to a printer that's right behind the desk on a credenza. Don't use the printer. It's noisy and slow. Just bring a floppy disk, copy what you need and get the hell out of there."

Dev was doodling. "Are you going to give me the magic words now?"

"Impatient little devil, aren't you, Devlin ? The will is under a simple file reference. Sliver\Tyler\Will. I told you the original will went back to Franklin Trust and, as far as I know, there are only two copies. One in my computer and one in Medford's. He always files important documents himself in his own computer. Obviously, you won't change anything in the file once you've got your copy. Oh, one other thing. The security guard likes to relax in the executive wing. It's usually the quietest spot on the floor. If you see him, his name is Ernie and he's always complaining about his feet."

"What do I do if I bump into him, give him a bunion pad?"

"Pray you don't bump into him, but don't worry about that too much. He doesn't know all the partners by sight. What can I tell you? Goodbye and good luck." Evie hung up.

Tess slowly pulled herself out of the chair, holding her back with her left hand and the desk with her right, and stretched. "Well, Dev, I hope you look good in stripes."

"Not bad, but I prefer plaid."

"Listen, wise guy, you are preparing to go into someone's office, after normal business hours, without notifying him, rifle through a computer and copy private documents."

Dev had an appealing grin. "Right. Piece of cake."

Tess settled back into the chair again. "Piece of cake, huh ? You're gonna need a very large piece of cake. With a file in it. Sounds like breaking and entering to me."

Devlin pointed to Medford's file on his desk. He ceremoniously opened it, pulled a one page letter and held it up for Tess to see.

"This, little mother, is what is commonly known in our profession, as a letter of authorization to review documents. You will note that it is duly and properly executed by my client, the honorable Addison Grant Medford, the turd."

Devlin's grin broadened. "Breaking and entering? Nah. I'm a title officer. It's called research."

Chapter 9

DEVLIN was on the Atlantic City Expressway at ten fifteen. He wasn't speeding. The last time he pushed the Black Demon to one ten mph, the troopers picked him up and Holenka went through hoops to keep Devlin's license from being revoked. He had been careful since that crazy night. Mom said he was never careful enough. But how much attention did she ever pay to me anyway? If she wasn't worrying about the old man, it was running to Mass to see Danny, or showing pictures of Kevin and the grandchildren to the neighbors. And there was always Aunt Nora. Uncle Bob and Nora were more on her mind than I ever was. Okay, now there are more reasons to be careful. There's my daughter and maybe, maybe, me and Mag.

The signs for the Ben Franklin were ahead. The clock on the Demon's black dashboard glowed and showed ten past eleven. He crossed the bridge, picked up the Vine Street Expressway and felt the tight knot in his stomach. Relax, Dev, there's a lot more than big bucks on the line. This ain't the casino or the hundred yard dash. Stay cool.

There was minimal traffic. He was in Center City by eleven-twenty, earlier than Evie said. He drove around the block, north of Market, past Penn Center and parked at Fifteenth and Chestnut at eleven-thirty on the nose. Devlin carefully studied the map of the office layout, looked at himself in the mirror, smoothed his hair, straightened his tie, grabbed the briefcase off the front seat and headed for the building.

He took a deep breath and pushed through the revolving door. SHIT!!! A tall black security guard was standing in the lobby. Sure glad Evie wished me luck. He entered the lobby and smiled at the guard while glancing at the badge on the uniformed chest.

"Hey, Eddie, did you see Mr. Medford come down yet?"

"You just missed him. Went by here about five minutes ago."

Devlin, you are a lucky devil. What a meeting that would have been. "Well, I better go up and burn some of the midnight oil while you relax down here." He headed for the elevator.

Eddie wagged a finger at him. "Don't complain. You're young, you got the energy. Wait till you get to be my age."

The elevator door closed noiselessly. Dev wiped his brow and hummed, "We're having a heat wave." Eighth floor. Baby, if it went any higher I'd get the bends. There's the men's room. Maybe there's some traffic I can hook on to.

The men's room door opened as Devlin approached it briskly. A young man of about twenty-six, with neatly combed black hair parted in the middle, snapped one of his suspenders and held the door for Devlin. Devlin hastily sipped from fountain and joined the young man.

"Thanks, I'm just grabbing some water. I'll go back in the office with you. You in litigation?" Dev asked, as he wiped his mouth.

"No. Bankruptcy. You?"

"I thought you were one of the new litigators. I'm in real estate. Finishing up a contract tonight. See you."

Devlin watched him walk away and smilcd in relief when he disappeared into the left hallway. He headed to

Evie's desk. The map was perfect. He found it easily. The eagle has landed. His heart skipped a beat. Where the hell is the computer? It was nowhere in sight. The top of the bare credenza showed traces of the absent printer's outline. Four round dots where the legs had sat were the only remaining evidence. Perfect. The eagle has landed and laid an egg. Now what? Better call Evie.

He could call from Evie's desk, but he preferred more seclusion. Ernie, the security guard, might show. The sign on the door next to him read Addison Grant Medford III. Devlin entered the darkness. Two high windows facing Chestnut offered enough light to lead him to the phone and see the eyes of General Grant's statue peering down. Devlin felt a chill.

He dialed Evie's number. His fingers felt strangely stiff. This guy Medford is haunting me. Evie answered. He covered the mouthpiece and whispered.

"It's me."

"Where are you? Have you got it?"

"I haven't got it and I'm in Medford's office."

Evie gasped. "What are you doing in Medford's office? Dammit, didn't you pay attention? I told you it's in the computer on my desk."

"The computer that *was* on your desk and the printer that *was* on the credenza, ain't. Now what?"

Devlin stood there in the silence, waiting for her answer and loosened his tie. If they catch me I'll have enough other tight stuff around my neck. He patted the briefcase holding the letter of authorization. Evie, where the hell are you. Better not shout at her. Could wake up the cleaning people.

"Evie, come on. . . ."

"Okay, okay, you got into the office. Let's not waste it. We'll try to get *his* copy. Sit down at his desk and turn on his computer. The switch is right under the screen on a power monitor. It's the button farthest to the right, marked *Master*. DON'T TURN ON THE LIGHTS IN THE

ROOM!"

"Relax, relax, I didn't. I'm working off the light coming in from the windows."

"Good. If the lights were on, Ernie would walk in for sure. You can do what we want off the light from the screen. Tell me when you're set."

Devlin sat in Addison Medford's chair. He felt the chill of the man's presence and hated it. He cradled the phone on his shoulder, turned on the power and listened to the hum of hardware warming up. God knows what secrets this man has stored here. The screen cast off a bluish light that illuminated a small arc over the desk. Devlin saw the chess pieces, Medford's army, staring at him, daring him to move, to invade their master's domain. This man is bad news. I know it. "Okay, Evie, it's on. I'm at the C prompt. I got to Word Perfect. You said the will is in file, Sliver\Tyler\Will, right?"

"Right."

"Okay. The rest should be a snap. Shift F-10, to retrieve document." A message flashed back to terrorize him. ERROR FILE IS LOCKED. Enter password! Crap. "Evie, he locked it up, I can't get in." Devlin's entire back was bathed in sweat.

"You got me so upset yesterday, I forgot to tell you he has a password to protect entry. Don't get nervous now. We have a problem and we're going to solve it."

Devlin had been in corners before. Keep cool. No point giving her hell and telling her she should have given you the password along with the map of the office. Keep your cool, Dev. "What's the password? Do you know it?"

"Not exactly. But I once I heard him tell it to Oliver Stern. Stern wanted something in a hurry, Medford used it aloud and was bragging to the senior partner how witty the password was. Then he pointed to the statue of Grant behind his desk."

Devlin heard footsteps outside the door. Oh, brother. Looks like the ball game is over. A white-haired, stoop-shouldered man in uniform passed the doorway and settled into the chair at Evie's desk. Gotta be Ernie. He's found his nest to coop. Dev felt his throat constricting. This place was depressing him. It was hard to speak, especially in whispers. He covered the phone's mouthpiece to block his voice from carrying.

"Evie, I think Ernie just went to sleep in your chair, right outside the door." He thought he heard her gasp again. There was good reason. He might be in front of the district attorney on charges and Sara might be in more jeopardy.

"Dev, sit quietly for five minutes. Ernie is taking one of his cat naps. He falls asleep quickly and is a very heavy sleeper. Valerie, one of the word processors, told me he does it every night. His snoring is a big joke with the girls. But he gets up in about fifteen minutes. Let me talk to you, but don't answer. Not until you hear him cutting the zzz's. I think the password is Grant, or another variation of the General's name. While we're taking guesses, you can try different entries. I'll tell David to grab the encyclopedia, thank heaven we bought one for the kids, and look up U.S. Grant. While he's looking there, try these six in the following order. Grant, U.S. Grant, General U.S. Grant, Ulysses, Ulysses S. Grant and General Ulysses S. Grant. I think a number was also mentioned. If you hit it, give me a small grunt."

Devlin had written down the six variations of the name. He wiped the sweat off his palms on his trousers and went at it. Devlin's fingers flew over the keys. Two minutes. He tried them all. No luck. He thought he heard a beep at U S Grant. He also heard another noise. Ernie was out like light and snoring away.

"Evie, nothing. I tried them all. Ernie has gone beddy-bye. What the hell are we gonna do? We could be here all night – guessing. I was ready to take the chance, but I want a fair shake."

"David found something interesting that may be a key. In 1866 Grant was made the first commanding general of all the armies of the United States. Try 1866 US Grant and all the other combinations we tried before."

Devlin tried every mutation and modification. Nothing. He was ready to put his fist through the screen and smash the blinking ERROR refusal that mocked him. He'd shot put it out the window to the heavens, to the stars. TO THE STARS ! Wait, wait, wait. A general has stars. One, two, three, some four. His heart pounded with excitement. Come on baby, please, give me a break. For me and Sara. He tried all of the combinations of the words with the all the combinations of stars. Still nothing. One more shot. The year. He tried, 1866****. Bingo!!

He tried to be calm, but his voice betrayed him.

"Evie, I got it. It's 1866 four stars. I'm going to make the copy. This better be the right file or I'll burn your house down. Not until after it's renovated."

There it was. Big white letters on a blue background. Tyler Will. "Cancel your fire insurance, Evie, you got that one right." The floppy went in. The little light flashed on and off, along with a beep that was music to his ears, bringing words and information for his family that might save a most precious life. Done. At last, the eagle had truly landed.

"Got it. Love ya, Evie. I'll call you tomorrow after I print it."

He carefully placed the floppy in his briefcase. Ernie was just getting up as Devlin passed him. Devlin stopped at the door and turned to see Ernie rubbing his eyes.

"Hey, Ernie, how the feet holding up?"

Ernie yawned and smiled. Must be a new kid with the firm.

Dev headed the Black Demon home. No. He would never sleep tonight until he read the will. He looked in the mirror and smiled at himself. The first order of the night is to slow down. You're so wired up right now, kiddo, you could light up Cleveland. Relax. Don't speed. You kept your cool, never blew it and did a good job. He rubbed his chin. Need a shave. Don't run away from what you're thinking, Dev. When someone else gives you a compliment, you are uncomfortable, but it's okay to pat your own shoulder.

He drove to his office in Linwood at a reasonable pace. Sinatra was on the radio and that was perfect. Old Blue Eyes sang "My Way." Dev whistled it as he turned on the office lights and the computer. It took less than two minutes for the printer to warm up and the will to be printed.

It took much longer for Devlin to be finished with it. Not the reading of it. It was only a single page. It was comprehending the mind of Jeremiah Tyler, the man who commanded the will to be written over a hundred years ago. Tomorrow he would read it to Maggie. Sara should be there too. She's a Tyler and old enough to understand. Will she understand how much she is affected by this ancient last will and testament? It might be a good idea to invite Frankie Holenka as well.

Jeremiah Tyler was one of the earliest settlers on Absecon Island. Born in 1804 on the mainland, he was drawn to the beaches along the sea that are now known as Atlantic City. He also enjoyed the hunting. In those years, the great portion of the island was sand-hills, dunes, ponds, swamps and thickets that were nesting places for the wild fowl. There was an abundance of game to be had. Very few who hunted had guns, but the wild fowl were so numerous they could be killed with clubs or captured with poles with hooks attached to the ends.

Tyler earned his living at odd jobs, often helping Jeremiah Leeds reap and harvest the grain. Leeds was the first settler of Absecon Island, the largest land owner and a man that young Jeremiah Tyler wished to emulate. He did so in many ways.

In 1826, in the week of his twenty-second year, Jeremiah Tyler married Ellen Latham. She brought him, as part of her dowry, the "Latham Tract." This two hundred and forty acre farm would be the beginning of their vast land holdings. The Tylers farmed, bred cattle, and for a time ran *The Atlantic House,* a tavern to serve the growing oyster trade and fishermen. They were prudent and industrious. They prospered; their savings grew and were invested with regularity in more land. By 1835, Jeremiah and Ellen Tyler had the largest land holdings on Absecon Island, second only to the Leeds family.

The Tylers had two children, both born late in their marriage, a pattern of birth that followed the family for generations. Their son, Robert, was born when Ellen was thirty-five. Daughter, Anne, born three years later, died of diphtheria at the age of ten. The family wealth flourished during the ensuing decades, allowing them to maintain their position of prominence in social and charitable circles.

In 1927, Benjamin Tyler, Jeremiah's grandson, moved his wife and infant daughter, Ellen, who had been named after her great-grandmother, to Margate. But wherever the family moved, they retained their identity to the Island, along with their rock bound ties to the church. Morality was the eleventh Tyler commandment, as inbred as the original ten. The virtues of righteousness had been repeated by the head of the household with unremitting regularity. The doctrine had passed from Jeremiah to his son, Robert, to his grandson Benjamin, to his great granddaughter, Ellen, to his great-great-granddaughter, Margaret. A reprint of the old laws still hung on the wall in Ellen's house in Margate.

> ***By the order of Lord Cornbury, 1704***
> *"The observance of the Lord's day is required, by abstaining from all servile work, unlawful recreations and unnecessary traveling; and any disorderly conduct will be punished by confinement in the stocks, imprisonment or whipping."*

Adultery was the most heinous, thc most unforgivable sin. The descendants of Jeremiah knew his feelings well. If it had been up to him, Hester Prynne would not have been the last transgressor to wear the scarlet A. This philosophy had survived in his will. The old man's remains lay quietly interred, but now, over a century later, his hand reached out from the grave and threatened the life of his great-great-great-granddaughter.

Chapter 10

THEY all had come in separate cars and met at 59 Berkley. Devlin, Maggie and Holenka. Sara had waited at 61, hesitant to return to her home alone. She and Jamie, holding hands, stood at the front door. Dev came to greet her, she walked to him; Jamie followed with bright, shining eyes.

"Good morning, girls. Jamie, this is family business, so you'll have to excuse us."

"I understand, Dev. I just wanted to say good morning. Oh, hi, Maggie."

With a farewell glance at Dev, Jamie slowly returned to her house as the others went to 59. Sara skirted the charred and jagged driveway, cautiously mounted the front steps and stopped at the closed door. She gave Dev the key. He entered first. Sara lingered, allowing Maggie and Holenka to precede her. The three waited inside, but Sara did not follow. Maggie retreated, put her arm on Sara's shoulder and led her in. The living room still held the odor of gasoline and burnt rubber. They sat tentatively around the dining room table. Sara looked at Trish's half finished knitting, bit her lip and stifled a sob as the ghosts surrounded her. Maggie tightened her arm about her daughter's shoulder.

"Honey, do you want to leave? We could do this some place else."

"No, no, no. It's better here. I don't want to sleep here yet, but. . . .I'm okay. Go ahead, Dev, read it."

Devlin looked at the lovely young girl and was filled with pride.

"Maggie, Sara, I wanted both of you to hear this at the same time. The reason I wanted Frank here will be obvious after you've heard it. Sara, I told Maggie about Frank and you should know this too. I've known him since I'm eight. He is one of my brother Danny's oldest and best friends and I would trust him with my life. He happens to be the captain of detectives of the Atlantic City police and they may be important to us. Okay. The will."

He cleared his throat and opened the envelope. They watched intently.

"I, Jeremiah Tyler, being of sound mind and body, do make this my last will and testament."

Dev stopped and ran his finger, line by line, over half the page.

"I'm not going to read all the descriptions of the property and other references, I think it's more important that I read the last paragraph. That's the one that affects this generation. Us. I mean, Maggie and Sara."

Sara bit her fingernail and Maggie's eyes turned downward to the dining table.

Dev continued, "As it has been the custom and goal of my life to follow the words of the Lord and the intent of the holy scripture, it is now my earnest wish that my property shall be so bequeathed upon my death. Therefore, all of my heirs, or my children's heirs, shall be only of Tyler bloodline. However, should any heir, or the descendant of any heir, have a child out of wedlock, the sinning parents of such child shall forfeit any right, title and interest to any Tyler property. The sins of the parents should not be visited upon the innocent child who is guilty of no wrong doing and should not suffer from their transgressions. Therefore, any inheritance involving properties of any kind, which would have been bequeathed to these sinners, shall instead pass to the guiltless descendant. If the child should die BEFORE reaching the age of legal majority, my estate shall be distributed as follows:

"1. All unimproved land shall pass to the city and be used as park lands for all the citizens of Absecon Island.

2. Any property that has been improved with a building shall pass to the occupant, thereby allowing the benefits of those improvements to stay with a worthy citizen, as opposed to a sinner who has lost all rights.

3. Should the child die AFTER reaching the age of majority and be without a natural heir of Tyler blood, all the property, both improved and vacant, shall go to the largest orphanage then existing in the great state of New Jersey.

Signed on this 5th day of July, 1851. Jeremiah A. Tyler, Witnessed by Thomas Latham."

Devlin lay the will on the table, folded his hands and waited for the questions that he knew would follow. Did they understand the implications of this? Holenka did, but he remained silent, allowing the others to speak before he did. Maggie scowled and was first.

"My great-great-grandfather must be pleased as all get out, throwing his moral thunderbolts and endangering our lives. Does this mean what I think it does? That the piece of ground that we asked two million for - that and everything else, like the house on Thurlow and cottage, all go to Sara?"

Maggie turned quickly to Sara.

"Honey, I don't mean it the way it sounds. I'm going to take care of you. I promise"

Sara was confused and looked to Devlin for an explanation, for wisdom. She felt orphaned again. Dev, a conversational policeman, held up his hand. He directed his answer to Maggie.

"What it means, Maggie, is just what you said. Everything that was going to you when your mother died, now goes to Sara. You, or we, are her guardians, till she is of age, which in the state of New Jersey, is eighteen."

Holenka pushed his chair from the table and stood.

He slapped at his stomach and shook his head at Devlin.

"There is more to this story, isn't there, Bobby?"

Devlin nodded.

"What?" asked Sara.

Holenka looked at Devlin again and raised his eyebrows in question. They understood one another without words. Devlin shook his head. His eyes sent the message to his friend. You better tell her. I don't want to. Holenka faced the two women.

"The will clearly states that if the innocent child, Sara, dies, the property, goes to him what put up a building on it. Mr. Devlin, our hot shot title man, is of the opinion that the building sitting on the sliver is The Palace Hotel. It is common knowledge that Mr. Maxwell Zeist is the owner of The Palace, in addition to a few other hotels in our neighborhood. You're asking two million for it. If Sara dies, The Max gets it for zilch. That sliver of land near Boardwalk seems to be the only property that's causing any car bombs in Atlantic County lately, right? That's about it, isn't it, Bobby?"

Now it was Sara who scowled. Devlin was sure he could read her mind this very minute. This kid of mine has my temper and the Tyler's love of a buck. Sara directed her explosion at Holenka.

"You mean he could get my property for nothing?"

Maggie smiled at her Tyler daughter. "That's right. But, he's not going to get our property, especially for nothing. That's a pretty big hotel to move off of our land. Maybe two million is too little to ask."

"You're darn right it is. My property is worth more than that." Sara was getting herself into the auction. "Did you see those ruts in the driveway, from the bomb. It was me they were after." She stopped suddenly, shocked with the realization of her statement. "I get so mad when I think of what they did to Trish and Alex."

Dev stroked her arm. "Sara, my old basketball coach, Whitey Neuman, used to say, 'Don't get mad, get even.' "

Sara nodded and contemplated the facts. "The will said he only gets my land if I die before I'm eighteen. I'll be eighteen in twenty days. What happens then?"

Maggie was quick with the answer. "Then it's your inheritance. He gets nothing and we can ask any price we decide. Or we can just tell him to move his hotel."

Sara and Maggie gazed at one another, both broke out in smiles that advanced to occasional laughter. Two girls at a pajama party over millions. They loved it. Holenka shrugged watching the greed spill over the dining room table. Sara grinned impishly, delighted with her conclusion. She rubbed her hands together.

"All the good things seem to happen when I'm going to be eighteen years old. So, I think we should ask for eighteen million."

"She ain't bashful," said Holenka.

"Makes a lot sense to me. That's *my* little girl," said Dev, and he also grinned.

"Why don't we just round it out to an even twenty million," said Maggie.

"You hear that, Frank," said Dev. "That's my *big* girl!"

Notifying Medford of the new asking price for the sliver was a buzz that Devlin wanted to enjoy at a face to face meeting. It was worth the drive to Philly. Now it was old hat. He knew the quickest route, where to park and, he knew Ernie, the night security guard. Devlin had Tess make the call. If he was going to see Mr. Big Shot, he would also act like one.

Mr. Devlin had vital news for. Mr. Medford. Mr. Medford would make himself available, if Mr. Devlin would come over at any time this afternoon. He'll be there. It will be a pleasure.

It was déja vu for Dev whcn he got to the Packard building and took the elevator to the eighth floor. The reception desk at Stern, Bradford and Altschuler had the same bouquet of flowers that was there a night ago. Today he had the opportunity to enjoy it. Must cost a bundle to change it weekly.

Mr. Devlin for Mr. Medford, he's expecting me, don't bother, I know the way.

Who's the new girl at Evie's desk? Ms. Walsh. She led him into the sanctum sanctorum. The lair of the big man on campus. Medford stood to greet him. Five foot six at best. Christ, the guy couldn't make guard for Girl's High. Better sit and not embarrass him. He's nervous. Good. Let's cut right to the chase.

"Before we go any further, Mr. Medford. . . ."

"Addison. Remember, my friends call me Addison."

Devlin gave him a smile. No shit, he's actually got a friend.

"Addison, I feel confident we can work this matter out, that I can be of service to you, as discussed. But the new information that we are now both aware of puts me in a position of a conflict of interest."

Medford smiled in return. "How so?"

Devlin ripped off a gorgeous smile. The guy is cool, but I think I'm one up on the smiling. Now for the fun. "You had previously instructed me to offer fifty thousand dollars for the purchase of the sliver you needed to clear your title problems."

Medford jumped right in. "I didn't say we needed. I said we preferred it for simplicity."

Devlin raised his index finger daintily. God, I'm so polite!

"May I finish please?" He paused to enjoy watching Medford's left eye twitch. What's the matter, counselor, can't take the heat when the tables are turned?

"As I was saying. Here I was, offering fifty thousand, and not even to the right owner. The party, that we both now know inherits under a will with some unusual provisions, is a young lady named Sara M. Johnson. Your client, Maxwell Zeist, could surely accommodate her asking price."

Medford didn't bat an eyelash. "Maxwell Zeist? Why do you bring him up?"

"You do represent him, don't you, Addison? It sure as hell seems that Sara's death would solve a helluva of lot of his problems. With her gone, The Max would get quite a windfall wouldn't he?"

"What will? Exactly what is it, you are referring to? If you have properly checked the record, as I have, I don't believe you will find any filed document that even vaguely refers to your allegations."

"You mean the will isn't recorded? Oh, fudge! Somebody must have slipped up. Not a problem. You've got a copy, counselor, and you're a lawyer. My goodness, you can cure that minor oversight. Record it, so it's available to the world and not hidden in the vault at Franklin Trust."

Medford leaped up. Three chess pieces fell on their sides. "Did Evie Conroy supply you with a copy of that document?"

Devlin sat calmly, admired the statue of U.S. Grant that he hadn't seen so clearly in the darkness during his last visit to this room, and brought an innocent gaze back to Medford's increasingly twitching eye.

Devlin's indifference infuriated Medford. How dare this two bit delivery boy ignore him. Medford's jaws clenched his teeth with the strength of a python. The pressure of the bite brought pain to his ear. He ignored it and continued.

"Yes, Mr. Devlin, I do represent Maxwell Zeist. And in that capacity, I can categorically assure you that under no circumstances would Mr. Zeist, or this office in any of its capacities representing Mr. Zeist, condone, endorse or join in any violent or criminal acts. Certainly not the bombing that you are alluding to."

"What bombing? I didn't mention any bombing."

Now it was Medford's turn to be mute. He slipped

into such an obvious trap of admission. His face reddened.

Devlin leaned back in his chair and almost felt sorry for Medford. Kick him off his throne and the little runt has no place to go. "Okay, Addison, Zeist is lily white and I heard your CYA speech."

"CYA?"

"Yeh, cover your ass. Now being that you do represent The Max, I'd like you to deliver a message to him."

The pain in Medford's ear became intense. He bit his tongue to divert himself. "I'm listening."

"Zeist wants to buy the sliver of land. Agreed. He's got it. Prepare all the closing documents and have all copies Federal Expressed to my office. You're never going to see the sellers. Somehow you've got them a little nervous. We're closing in escrow. I'll get the signatures and have them notarized. Tess Donahue of my office will inform you which attorney will handle it. And, Addison old boy, up till now you wanted to leave the price blank. Now you can fill it in. It's an even twenty million. Be in touch, Addie."

Devlin waved goodbye and exited the room as Medford sank to his chair, defeated, for one of the few times in his life. Through his open door he could see the despised Devlin stop to nod to Ms. Walsh and her eagerness to respond.

When Devlin disappeared from view, Medford called Ms. Walsh, demanding her instantaneous attention. Ms. Walsh, a full figured, single woman of thirty-eight responded immediately. She needed the employment more than Evie Conroy had. Office gossip informed her of the suddeness of Evie's dismissal, and the demands of working for Addison Medford.

"If you've finished socializing with Mr. Devlin, I'd like you to take some dictation."

Ms. Walsh entered promptly with her steno book, sat in the chair next to his desk, pencil poised for the assignment. Medford closed his door, walked back to the front of the desk, sat on its edge and leaned toward her. He gazed at the brimming breasts that filled the V of her blouse. She averted her eyes. His voice was soft and pleading. Though she had only been there a week and knew its sound, the timbre now, was curiously unfamiliar.

"Do you find Mr. Devlin attractive?"

Ms. Walsh was taken by surprise. She was confused and wished to retreat.

"Well, I. . . .I don't really know him, Mr. Medford."

He waited silently, demanding her answer. She focused on her steno book. "Yes, he is attractive. He is quite handsome."

Medford straightened abruptly and returned to his chair. He could disapprove of Devlin alone without the unneeded endorsement of the likes of Ms. Walsh.

"Never mind the dictation now. I'll call you in later. Shut the door and keep yourself available for the rest of the afternoon."

She left hurriedly. Medford required a return to familiar, charted waters. He called Zeist to inform him of the latest demands. He also wanted to be assured that Zeist was not in any way behind the car bomb. Was it Trentino? Which client should he support? Which client paid more fees? Zeist came to the phone.

"Max, I'm glad you're available. I just had a meeting with that Devlin. He's definitely in with the Crandall woman. He's read the will and suspects you were behind the bombing."

"Is he crazy? You know I would never be involved in stupidity like that."

"That's exactly what I told him."

"I'm telling you, Addison, it's that lunatic Trentino."

"You may be right. I also called about the sliver."

"Good. Is it settled? Is the contract prepared yet? Don't do one of your forty hour jobs and delay it."

"I'm not delaying anything. The price was not resolved. They're now asking twenty million."

Zeist whistled. He was accustomed to dealing in tens,

hundreds of millions, but a price jump of two million to twenty million had his attention. "That son-of-a-bitch Devlin did tip her off."

A heartfelt smile, the first in months, spread on Medford's face. Zeist could see Devlin for what he was. It was good to have an ally in his enmity for Devlin.

"That's not the worst of it, Max. When Trentino finds out, we'll have a loose cannon on our hands.'

Maxwell Zeist thumbed through the prospectus of his two hundred million dollar financing and came to the Contingency section. Thirty million was set aside. This was a contingency he would have to live with.

"Accept the price and close the deal. We need a clean title, we need that damn sliver and I will not jeopardize the bond financing."

"You read the will."

"Of course I read it. You showed it to me." Zeist scribbled twenty million on his embossed stationery. Half was his. "Addison," he said, slowly, musically breaking the name into syllables, "where is your friend Trentino?"

"I'll be seeing him tomorrow. To tell him about the new asking price. Shall I complete the contract?"

"Wait forty-eight hours."

Chapter 11

NINETEEN days to Sara's birthday. Holenka received the Federal Express package from Herb Lederer, assistant Attorney General of the State of New Jersey, at nine thirty in the morning. It was good to have friends in high places. Lederer had answered Holenka's questions in a well organized three page memo, red lined and paper clipped the pertinent sections of the one hundred twelve page document. Holenka called another meeting at 59 Berkley. He said it was important. They were all there by eleven.

Holenka, the only one who took a different seat, placed himself at the head of the dining room table. They all must understand the urgent need for action. He held up the document.

"This is a copy of a prospectus that has been filed with the state A.G.'s office. There are a few familiar names in it, and one you haven't heard before."

Sara raised her hand. Holenka repressed a smile and nodded for her to proceed.

"Does this have anything to do with the will? With my property?"

"In my opinion, yes. I think it all ties in with the attack. Listen closely and try to follow me. A corporation named Emzee Hotel Holdings has filed this prospectus offering to sell two hundred million dollars of twelve and half percent bonds. These high yield junk bonds will be secured by a mortgage on all the Emzee Hotel Holdings, which include three hotels in Atlantic City, two hotels in the Caribbean and a New York office building. One of the hotels in AC is The Palace. I'd say it's a pretty good guess that Emzee stands for Maxwell Zeist, who just happens to be the controlling shareholder. The Max, our first familiar name. Are you all following me so far?"

Sara shook her head, Maggie shrugged and Devlin nodded yes. Holenka permitted himself a small smile. The hot shot title officer was with it.

"Let me jump to the part that I think affects you three the most. The document was filed by Stern, Bradford and Altschuler; Addison Grant Medford III, attorney for the firm. Our second familiar name. A consortium of Wall Street and European investment bankers are underwriting the issue and the word on Wall Street is the deal's a shoo-in, especially if the State of New Jersey passes the referendum to guarantee the principal. With high interest for the investors and big commissions for the salesmen, the bonds will sell like hotcakes. The Casino Bond referendum is being strongly recommended by our esteemed Lt. Governor, Charles Everett Radcliff, the bosom buddy of our busy Mr. Zeist. Radcliff. Our third familiar name. The power boys are ready to have a party and pop open the champagne, but there is one little hitch."

Devlin interrupted without raising his hand. "They need clear title."

"Bingo! Go to the head of the class," said Holenka. "It could be a problem, but they know that money can solve any problem. This wise, experienced and incredibly well connected little group have set up a Contingency Fund of thirty million dollars. That should be enough to solve a bucket full of problems."

Sara grinned as Maggie raised her hand.

"It seems that my suggestion to ask for twenty million was a good one. If they pay what we're asking, they'll still have ten million left in their Contingency Fund and Zeist can close his deal."

Holenka stood to his full height, stretched and slapped his stomach.

"That's right, Mag. They'll have ten million left, but they started out with thirty. That's a big chunk of dough to drop for a small piece of land. An important question is, who's paying the twenty? Is it all coming out of Zeist's pocket, or is anyone else getting hurt?" He held up Lederer's memo. "According to Section Twelve, subsection Aii, the unexpended funds of the Contingency Fund, do not all go to Emzee Hotel Holdings. Emzee gets fifty percent, and the other fifty percent goes to Brandywine Capital Corp."

Holenka stopped, returned to his seat and delivered his next statement in low deliberate tones. "It looks like Brandywine is paying part of the freight."

He directed his next statement to Devlin. "To the tune of ten million. So, I ask Herb Lederer, who is Brandywine? One hundred percent of the stock of Brandywine Capital Corp. is owned by Rocco Davino, the father-in-law of Alphonse Vincenzo Trentino. A payment of twenty million to Sara would cost Little Vinnie half. He'd kill his mother for ten million."

Holenka saw Sara quiver and the grim expression on Maggie's face. Devlin's eyes hardened and he spoke first.

"The car bomb. You think it's him, not Zeist?"

"I told you before, Bobby, it's not Zeist's style. But it sure as hell looks like Trentino's style."

Maggie stood behind Sara's chair and put her arms protectively around the girl's shoulders. "What is wrong with you two? I don't care who is behind the attack. It's Sara that matters, it's Sara that we must protect."

"That's why I called this meet. We've got a time bomb on our hands. Sara must be secured until her eighteenth birthday. That's nineteen long days from now. I think the safest situation would be direct policc protection. Sara goes to a motel, we put on a twenty four hour detail until the heat's off."

Sara had absorbed it all with fascination. "Frank, I mean Mr. Holenka, you sound like one of the detectives on TV. But why can't I stay here? With Jamie and Mrs. Matthews? The police could watch us here."

So he was a TV detective? He wished he had their pay. "Sara, I don't think it's a good idea for you to stay with the Matthews or anywhere else in this neighborhood. The initial incident occurred at 59 Berkley, the Matthews live at 61. This is a known location to the perpetrator. Remaining here creates high exposure to unrelated parties. "

Sara knew the answer but had to ask the question. "Who are the unrelated parties "

Holenka stared at her with unblinking, unfeeling eyes. This kid better get the message. "Phyllis, Ed and Jamie Matthews."

Maggie hugged her daughter's shoulders harder. "Alright, Frank, you've made your point. She's not staying here and she's not staying next door. Where?"

Good. He had their attention. Holenka put his sunglasses on. "Your place or Dev's could be just as dangerous. That leaves the motel that I mentioned, or the station house."

Sara recoiled. "You mean I'd go to jail?"

Dev banged the table. "She's not going to any damn jail. And as for the police protection program, I've heard enough stories where that didn't work. And, how do we know we can trust our protectors? Who the hell knows what Medford told Zeist, or what Zeist told Radcliff, or what Radcliff told the state police? "

Sara huddled in her chair as Maggie gently stroked the girl's trembling shoulders.

"What do you think we should do, Dev?" asked Maggie.

"We have to hide, not in a motel, but somewhere they would never expect us to be. It isn't forever, it's only for nineteen days."

"Where? I heard these people can find you anywhere," said Maggie.

Holenka nodded. They sat in silence, each pondering a suitable sanctuary. The dining room clock chimed at eleven-thirty, startling them all. Devlin clapped his hands.

"We're looking for a place that is the least obvious, that we can get to easily, and that the police can get to quickly in case of emergency. And of course, it's got to be immediately available. I think we may have one. Frank, you remember Lennie Karp ? His old man had the deli on Tilton Road. We used to call Lennie 'the fish' because he always smelled from herring. He and his family moved to Florida, to Jupiter, but he bought a house on 23rd Avenue, in Longport, to spend the summers up here. It's empty until next July. I know he'd let me use it. Any hood looking for us would never figure we'd go there. It's near the end of the island, a dead end location with very few outlets."

"Who's going to stay with her, Bobby ?"

"I will," said Maggie.

"We both will."

Holenka shrugged. "You got a gun?"

"No. You know I don't have a gun, Frank."

"Well you sure as hell can't get a permit for one in less than nineteen days. If you had one, would you use it?"

Holenka and Devlin exchanged knowing looks.

"I won't break my promise to Danny."

"You wouldn't have to, you could call me. Are you going to make this decision all by yourself ?" asked Holenka.

Devlin looked at his daughter with loving concern. "No, Frank. We're a family, we're going to vote on it."

Maggie's hands were still on Sara's shoulders. Sara covered one with hers. She stared at Devlin with doubtful eyes. "Does my vote count the same way as yours and Maggie's?" she asked.

"It sure does, honey. Whattya say?"

Sara turned to look at Maggie. Maggie nodded. Sara looked back to Devlin, and then at Holenka, who remained stoic. Her voice was barely above a whisper. She couldn't risk Jamie's life. "Okay, me too. When will we leave?"

"As soon as I get the okay from Lennie," said Dev.

"Whenever you do it, make it after dark," said Holenka.

They exited 59 without further words. Sara, holding Maggie's hand, again dodged the scarred driveway. They stood grouped on the sidewalk, next to Holenka's car, hesitant to disband. Holenka rested his hand on Devlin's shoulder and addressed the two women.

"I want you to know that I love this guy, and I'm going to watch you three like a hawk. Bobby, when you're all set, let me know where you are." He drove away at a speed of twenty five, his arm out the window waving goodbye.

"I like Frank," said Sara.

"So do I," added Maggie. "You're lucky, Dev. You have real friends. What was the promise you made to your brother, Danny?"

Devlin's face lingered in the direction of Frank's departing car, watching it slowly turn off Berkley. He imagined Danny was in the car. The two of them, driving off, leaving him behind.

"I promised Danny I'd never take a human life. He made me promise on my. . . ."

After a minute of staring at Dev's back, Sara's curiosity needed satisfaction. "A promise on your what?"

Devlin faced her and stared deep into her eyes, hoping she would understand.

"On my immortal soul."

Maxwell Zeist didn't get his reputation for having the Midas touch, or the nickname of "The Max" idly. It took twenty-five years of unremitting effort, dedication, sacrifice and unwavering allegiance to the gods of success. Early in his beginnings, he had heard the old axiom, "It's not what you know, it's who you know." He had followed that advice devotedly for two decades, accumulated a circle of friends and relationships that included politicians, foreign royalty, statesmen, both here and abroad, the movers on Wall Street, foreign money connections in Europe, Asia and any other international money center that was emerging. This was in addition to his intimate and nodding acquaintance with the social leaders of New York and Palm Beach, the premier Hollywood and Broadway luminaries, stars, starlets, fashion models and beautiful women of little national note, but possessors of a myriad of talent in their own right.

Considering the size to which it ultimately grew, Zeist had started his empire modestly. At the age of twenty two, his maternal grandmother had left him a moderate inheritance. A six-family apartment building on Bryant Avenue in the East Bronx. The neighborhood had deteriorated and the building was half vacant. One night it burnt to the ground. Lucky Max. The fire insurance premiums were current, the loss proceeds far exceeded what he could have sold it for. After paying off the mortgage, there was eight thousand left. In the game he wanted to play, it wasn't much, but at least it was a beginning.

Even at that tender age, Max had an eye for a bargain. His small bankroll was insufficient to swallow what he saw, and what he saw, he wanted. Early in the game, Max realized he needed OPM. Other people's money. He became friendly with Len Carstel. Len was a year older than Max, but already had achieved the exalted station of junior loan officer at Old Stuyvesant Savings and Loan. An important position for such a young man. An invaluable contact for young Max.

It was 1973; he turned to the East Side of Manhattan. The Third Avenue El was down and development was advancing. His timing was exquisite. Max concluded that values would rise in this neighborhood. Others, with far more capital and experience than young Max, had come to the same conclusion. His unremitting drive and resourceful, imaginative mind sent him to the record rooms. He discovered that Marvin Daniels, a major New York City developer, was assembling the block front on 3rd Avenue between 71st and 72nd. A sixty foot plot would be needed to complete the full block assemblage. Rachel and Lou Zuckerman, the owners, who ran a small grocery store and lived in the back were holding out. The Zuckermans wanted one hundred and fifty thousand. He was seventy-eight and she was seventy-four. It was time to call it quits, but they wanted their price. The Daniels organization had not completed the purchase of the key larger parcel, and not yet in dire need of the Zuckerman plot. Daniels offered one hundred and ten thousand.

Young Max determined Daniels would need it sooner than later. He became a steady customer of the grocery store. He told Rachel Zuckerman about his grandmother, he told Lou about his ambitions, that his family had once been in the same business. Anything he thought they wanted to hear. Max had always been a charmer.

He offered the Zuckermans their full asking price of one hundred and fifty thousand, hoping, knowing, they would accept the five percent good faith deposit. Max smiled and pressed the check for seventy-five hundred into the old man's hand. It was just the one hundred forty-two thousand five hundred he was missing. He turned to his friend Len Carstel at Old Stuyvesant. They wouldn't lend him the funds he needed to close. He was too inexperienced, he did not have enough equity in the deal.

Max was frantic, his first big deal and it was slipping through his fingers. He pleaded with the old couple to give him a six month extension of the closing date. Somewhere he would get the necessary funds to close. Lou Zuckerman liked the young man, Max's family and his were fellow grocers. Rachel was already baking cookies for Max. They would give the ambitious youngster a six months extension. A few more months, what did it matter? They had been in the store for forty years, they could wait another six months.

As a matter of fact, the old man said, he would even give a year, if Max would increase the deposit to ten thousand. Zuckerman did want to be assured of a closing. After all, he was an old man.

Max returned to Len. Upon Len's recommendation and the assignment of the contract, the loan committee of Old Stuyvesant agreed to lend Max the additional twenty five hundred dollar deposit money. Within ten months, the Marvin Daniels Organization had completed all of their assemblages, with the single exception of the sixty foot plot that Max controlled. The Daniels Organization had obtained a sixty million dollar mortgage commitment from Metropolitan Life to build a luxury high rise on the full block. Max was elated when he read the press release in the New York Times, issued by the proud mortgage broker. Marvin Daniels' attorney made the offer of one hundred sixty thousand to Max. That was ten thousand more than the Zuckermans had wanted. Max had a ten thousand dollar deposit and could double his money.

That wasn't the game that Max had played. He now controlled the inside plot for the assemblage. Max demanded seven hundred and fifty thousand, and got it. In less than a year, he had made six hundred thousand on his seventy five hundred dollar investment. The story was published in many financial and real estate trade papers in addition to the Times. It was his first big deal and the beginning of the legend of The Max.

With the guidance of Len Carstel, whom Max wined, dined and nurtured, Old Stuyvesant provided sufficient funds for Max to mortgage out of every deal. Using this formula, with no further investment on his part, he leap-frogged to deals in the millions. Whenever financing left a gap and equity capital was required, "The Max," as he was now popularly known, turned to wealthy private investors. They flocked to him like oxen to the water hole. He had the Midas touch. It must be true, it said so in all the papers. He formed Limited Partnerships through his Wall Street contacts, who also brought him funds from international sources. A Saudi prince was a substantial and frequent investor.

Zeist had ready access to the ear of the President's Council of Economic Advisors and was privy to the leanings of the Federal Reserve. The current U.S. economy was seven trillion and still heating up. There was a great sensitivity to the specter of inflation. The Fed could react with still another rate increase, pushing up the prime, sending a flood of increased debt service costs across the nation, sweeping the borrowings of Emzee Hotel Holdings along with it. The ebbs and flows of interest rates are affected by many tides, and in the past, Zeist had been on target. His PR staff trumpeted his prescience. It attracted more investors. The legend of "The Max" grew; the man who pulled off the maximum on a deal. Everybody wants to ride with a winner.

Occasionally, even a winner must borrow. Borrowing is leverage. With a small lever, one can move a very large boulder. If, however, the lever breaks, the boulder may slide backwards and crush the borrower. Max understood this intimately in its every detail and nuance. Yet, in 1988 and 1989, he had borrowed heavily, pledging many of his assets, finally sliding dizzily into the one bad act that he had sworn never to commit. He signed his name personally against the entire debt. He had pushed everything on the table in one massive gamble, poised to be rewarded for this risk with his greatest triumph and wealth beyond all others. He would be number one in Forbes, the true Max.

Within eighteen months the global real estate market plunged into a precipitous downturn, the victim of its own excesses of over-building, speculation and poorly underwritten loans. Values in the U.S. plummeted at a rate similar to the Great Depression. Zeist regrouped. He negotiated, re-negotiated, wiggled out of squeeze after squeeze, calling on powerful friends to intercede when catastrophe seemed inevitable. He had stayed financially alive with wizardry and perseverance. He would not give up now. The market was turning for the better. The proposed two hundred million fund-raising would give him the vital breathing room he needed to stabilize his shaky empire and keep all intact.

It was mind-boggling for Max to think that the fortune he had created could crumble two decades later, because of a sliver of land no larger than the sixty foot plot in Manhattan he had started with. If he had to pay the Crandall woman the twenty million, if his half cost him ten, he would. But now, ten million was real money. Maybe Little Vinnie would solve his problems. Another call to Radcliff might be in order.

Chapter 12

IT had taken Devlin four long distance calls to locate Lennie Karp. He had given his personal permission immediately, but Dev still must wait. Lennie had to check with his folks. Dev moaned under his breath. The Fish is thirty-eight years old and still has to ask his mommy if a friend can sleep over. Another precious twenty-four hours lost. Finally the word from Mrs. Karp. The answer was yes. Any friend of Lennie's could use the house in Longport. But leave it clean. The key was under the whale shaped flower pot on the back porch with the geraniums. Her closing message. It wouldn't hurt if you watered the geraniums.

Maggie picked up Dev at ten minutes to midnight. The trunk of Maggie's Volvo was large enough for her clothes, Dev's, and, hopefully, Sara's. Dev had left the Demon at his house. The Corvette could seat only two. Now his family was three. They didn't speak on the ride to get their daughter. She was still with the Matthews; they wouldn't let her enter 59 by herself.

The three of them stood in the dimly lit living room, unsure of the next move. Maggie took Sara's hand and led her to the bedrooms stairs. "You better go up and get your things. Do you want me to go with you?"

Sara held the bannister and halted, removed her hand from Maggie's and waved her back. "No. No, I want to go by myself." In a cloak of silence, she warily ascended the carpeted stairs, releasing the bannister, her shoulder hugging the protective wall. Maggie wrung her hands and Dev's stomach tightened as they watched their daughter cautiously rise to meet the ghosts in the rooms above.

Midway on the landing she stopped, suspended in fear, returning to the echoes of a bomb blast that shattered her life along with those dearest to her. Perspiration trickled down the back of her neck, dampening her blouse. With a deep breath, she took another cautious step forward.

Dev agonized over her terror. He started toward her, but Maggie arrested his advance. Their eyes met in the shadows and held fast. They watched and waited, allowing their daughter to continue her journey. She reached the upper landing.

There were three bedrooms. The first, on the right, had been Trish's sewing room. They would never have a second child. Sara's room was at the end of the hallway, over the garage, the windows facing the driveway. The scarred, scorched driveway where fingers of flame and death had reached for her. She inched along the corridor to her room, closing her eyes to the one across the hall. She entered quickly, leaping to the familiar safety of the four walls she knew so intimately, shut the door and pressed her damp back against it. The moonlight shone through the window on White Bear, her teddy, sitting innocently on a shelf, its flat, unblinking, black eyes ignorant of the tragedy that had struck this house.

Sara turned on the light and looked about her. It was the same, yet it would never really be the same again. She assembled her clothing: sweatshirts, jeans, underwear, her Mainland High jacket and T-shirt, an extra pair of sneakers, no slippers, the Sleepless in Seattle and Rutgers nightshirts and a Hard Rock Cafe T-shirt. It all fit easily in the duffel bag from her closet. She raced past Trish and Alex's room with eyes clenched shut on her way to the bathroom for her toiletries. Toothbrush, hair blower, shampoo, clear nail polish and hairbrush. Back to her room. That was it. Her school books sat on her desk. She examined the stack, choosing English and Social Science. Who knows, maybe she'd survive this and graduate. The duffel bag was now heavy and fully loaded. A last look. She might never return and wanted a token, a proof of her existence. She tucked White Bear, untouched since her childhood, under her arm.

She advanced no further than one step, stopped in front of Trish and Alex's room and dropped her duffel to the floor. Sara and White Bear entered the room that she had run to with her first scraped knees. The hallway light cast shadows on the corners of the room where no one was hiding to surprise her with gifts. The unfinished embroidery lay on the dresser, next to Sara's picture. She sat on the edge of the bed, as she had done a thousand times before, and fell upon Trish's pillow, enveloped in the well loved scent. Her tears ran freely down the crevice where the head of the woman that nurtured her had lain. The muffled sobs were racked with pain as her anguish and suffering echoed down the hallway to Maggie and Devlin. "Please, please come back," she moaned. "I want you so much. Trish, please come back."

Dev started up the stairs. Maggie put her arm upon his and shook her head. The sobs continued, in heart rending groans. Maggie could not remain below.

"I'll go up to her," she said. Maggie quickly reached the bedroom, took the weeping young girl into her arms and kissed away the tears.

"Oh, Maggie, I miss them so much. It hurts me inside. They always asked me to call them Trish and Alex, because I wasn't theirs. But I was, I was, I was theirs. They were really my mom and dad."

"Of course, sweetheart, I know. I know only too well what it means to lose someone you love. My mother died this year. And when I lost you, gave you to Trish and Alex, I also gave up a part of myself. The one person I loved more than anyone in the world. I know I can never take the place of what Trish meant to you. I don't want to. But, I hope one day, you can forgive me enough to let me try to be the mother to you that I never was. We'll have time to talk about it in the next weeks. We'll be together for many hours. I won't say anything else now."

Sara nodded. Her breast heaved with unremitting sighs for her loss. Maggie felt her own heart would break. She helped the unhappy girl down the stairs and into the car. Dev loaded Maggie's Volvo and they were off to Longport. It would be the most precipitous fifteen days of Sara's life. Sara held White Bear to her face, clutching the tattered stuffed animal for dear life. Maggie gently patted the toy.

"I gave him to you for your third birthday. You called him White Bear."

Sara stared at Maggie. Was she the lady with the golden hair?

"I think I remember."

Dev drove the Volvo slowly, unaccustomed to its movement. They took the route down Shore Road to Longport Boulevard, across the Risley Channel bridge to Longport. Maggie watched the lights, woven to the Channel, reflect on the water, blinking a welcome. She prayed it promised safe harbor. They reached Nine 23rd Avenue at twelve forty-five in the morning. The house, a two bedroom ranch model, had the distinct advantage of an attached garage with a door into the house. Strange eyes need not see them walking to the street, getting in the car. Evil hands could not place a bomb in a car that was not parked outdoors. Dev had gotten there earlier that day, picked up the key and the remote garage door opener. There was excitement in the air as they groped in the darkness for the living room light. Dev found Maggie's waist and the urge to embrace her was irresistible. He didn't fight it. Neither did she. Sara discovered the light and her parents in each other's arms. They all laughed. It was a good beginning.

It was forty days to the New Jersey election. The polls showed Governor Charles Everett Radcliff leading by a margin of twenty eight percent. Zeist often reminded Radcliff, especially during their conversations of the New Jersey state guarantee of the Casino Bonds, Radcliff's campaign funds were triple that of his opponent. Voter approval would assure the ultimate sale of the entire two hundred million. An over-subscription would be an opportunity to increase the amount of the raise by another fifty or hundred million. Zeist would always find another place to invest the excess capital. His theory was consistent. If it's O.P.M., take it.

The presentation of the referendum was vital. The Max was a master of this domain. Massive state-wide marketing had been prepared and professionally executed, informing the public of the benefits of voting yes for Casino Bond approval. Newspaper ads, editorials, TV ads, bumper stickers, casino bus banners, billboards and all available media throughout the state promised, cajoled and signaled the voters of the benefits. There would be no cost to the public, only the borrower. The bonds would generate additional employment and taxes to the state, county and municipality. In addition, the well publicized improvements proposed in Atlantic City by The Max, would generate more construction jobs, which, in turn, would generate more revenue for local merchants and the spiral of an expanding, productive economy would continue for the Jersey shore. A vote against the Casino Bonds was *Unamerican!*

Zeist spoke daily with his PR and consulting firms. No angle to brainwash the public should be passed up. He read every report. Many voters do their homework and follow their predetermined decision on the issues in the privacy of the voting booth. Many others do not. Like shopping in the supermarket, they fall victim to last minute impulse decisions. Zeist had a stroke of genius. An average looking girl, surrounded by two stunning girls, is very often swept along on the triple date. Zeist's consulting firm verified this group reaction pattern. Zeist and Radcliff would exploit it. Part of the strategy was the format, and the ideal position in that format, the Casino Bond approval, would be placed on the ballot. Radcliff was implementing the plan. The idea might give them a landslide.

They would bury the Casino Bond approval in the *middle* of two other referendums that had received very popular support. Zeist suggested they offer the standard ballot punch for each referendum, plus a single ballot punch on the card encompassing all three issues. A universal "Yes" or "No" for all three referendums. It would confuse some voters who wanted to vote for two items and not the Casino Bonds. Zeist reviewed the matter with his marketing consultants and the conclusion was clear. Unsure voters would either vote "Yes" because they wanted the Parkland Bond, an incredibly attractive package that Zeist would make more appealing, or the voter would abstain. Abstaining was acceptable. As long as the ballot wasn't "No," thereby giving the "Yes" voters more leverage. Zeist called Radcliff for a progress report when he was alone in his office. These moments were best in seclusion.

"Charley, how's the package looking?"

"I must say, Max, it looks prettier in print than I even hoped for."

Max stroked his hairline moustache with his thumb and forefinger and admired his reflection as it stared back at him in the mirror covered wall. He was getting a bit grey, but it was growing in nicely around the temples. Rather distinguished, like Gregory Peck. "Read it to me."

"We're setting it up like this. We're putting the increase of the Homestead rebate, obviously the most popular, first. Then ours, the Casino Bond. Third, the Parkland Bond. There will be extensive explanation on the Parkland issue so they'll see how attractive it is and we can leave them with a smile."

Zeist was in paradise when involved in these discussions. Medford liked to piddle with his little chess pieces, but this was the great American public. Cajole, appeal, manipulate. That's why they come to my casino. "Read the details on the Parkland."

"It's lengthy, but here's the gist of it. The Parkland Bonds of six million are approved only if fifty percent of the costs are contributed by the private sector. If the private sector does not contribute three million, the taxpayers pay zero."

The Max smiled broadly. "My consulting firm has completed a telephone poll in fifteen of the twenty-one counties. Voters love the Parkland Bonds because the perception of the little guy is that Mr. Moneybags will have to spring for the costs. I think I may be one of their white knights and make a sizeable contribution."

"You're beautiful, Max. Your PR boys will eat that one up with a spoon."

"Don't be modest, Charley, you're a great help. I couldn't do any of this without your guidance. Keep me posted and have a grand weekend. Oh, speaking of weekends, if you can scoot over to The Palace anytime late Saturday afternoon, there is a charming singer I'd like you to meet."

Radcliff looked at his calendar and angrily flicked a finger at a page. "Love to, but my in-laws are coming in from Michigan. They want to be here during the election to give me moral support. Probably will stay until New Year's. But, maybe I could – better forget it. I'll keep you posted. Bye, Max."

The Max swiveled in his chair. He was feeling lucky again. He would tell the PR boys to announce a million dollar pledge to the Parkland Program tomorrow. If they needed more, he might even do that. It was only a pledge, not cash. Who knows, maybe Vinnie Trentino would save him ten million and a million would be peanuts.

At seven-fifteen in the morning Grey Eyes was parked at the beginning of Berkley. At six he had already finished his coffee at the Greek diner, rechecked Sea Garden and Highland, the side streets on either side of Berkley as possible emergency exits after he did the job. They were no good. Both dead end. He would have to leave by foot. He hated that. Being boxed in was shit. The first time he was caught was at the dead end of an alley behind a fur store he was heisting. He was sixteen-years-old. A year younger than the girl. He got four years in juvenile, was out in twenty-two months and figured he had learned a lot.

Seven-forty. The other girl, the Matthews kid, not his mark, came out to get the paper. He had the car parked at an angle so she couldn't spot the plates. Nice T-shirt, but the blonde's got better legs. He loved them long. Clear up to a young ass. He watched her unfold the paper and go back into the house. Nobody else showed. He waited fifteen more minutes and knew something was wrong. His gut told him.

When he was twelve-years-old, two kids, about fourteen, stopped him to ask directions. They needed money for a phone call. Without a word, he knew they were lying. He could smell it. He stabbed the taller one in the hand with an ice pick and laughed as the other ran, pissing in his pants. He had made his bones at twenty and now had all the finely tuned instincts of a professional killer.

He eased his car by 61, saw nothing to make him stop and drove around the corner to the pay phone on Shore Road. He wouldn't call from his car. Traceable. Jamie answered. He covered the mouthpiece of the phone with a handkerchief and lowered the register of his voice.

"Good morning, I'm sorry to bother you so early. This is Sergeant McNamara. We're continuing the investigation of the car bombing and something came up this morning that needs an immediate answer. Is Sara up yet? I have to speak to her. It will only take a minute."

Jamie looked about the kitchen. Her father was in the shower and her mother in the basement with the laundry. Sara had told her not to speak to anyone about the move. But this was the police. "Wait a minute, Sergeant, I'll get my mother."

"No! You don't want to involve your mother. It might not be safe. Especially with this new information. Just call Sara to the phone."

Jamie bit her lip in agitation. Her mother could be hurt. What was happening? Why didn't Sara confide in her and tell her what this was all about? "I'm sorry, Sergeant McNamara, but Sara is gone. She won't be back for a while. I don't know what else to tell you. You won't have to speak to my mother now, right?"

"Right. We'll find Sara and get the information directly from her. You can just forget about the call. Have a good day, miss."

Jamie struggled to hang up the phone as her mother appeared in the kitchen with a loaded laundry basket. Phyllis saw her daughter's ashen face and the shaking hand that held the receiver. "Who was that? Did someone call just now? I thought I heard the phone ring."

"No, Mom, it was nothing. The phone didn't ring." Jamie saw her mother's eyes narrow and knew her answer was unaccepted. She tried again. "It was a wrong number."

The car bomb was still fresh in Phyllis Matthews' memory. She pushed the laundry basket to the sink, ignoring the large box of Tide that slipped to the floor and grasped her daughter by the shoulders. "Jamie Matthews, you tell me what that call was about. I can see it written all over your face. This is no time for girlish pranks."

Jamie blushed and blurted it out. "He wanted to talk to Sara. He said he was Sergeant McNamara, from the police. Oh, Mom, do you think I got Sara in trouble?"

Phyllis dialed the Linwood police. "Hello, this is Phyllis Matthews, may I please speak to Sergeant McNamara; he just called me."

The officer at the desk advised her that there was no McNamara on the force. Perhaps, he suggested, she should try one of the other nearby towns. But as far as he recalled, there was no one named McNamara there either. She thanked him and asked him to have Lt. Baines call her. No problem, the Lieutenant would be in at ten. Phyllis searched her purse for Frank Holenka's card.

Grey Eyes checked his watch. Seven fifty-four. Did she skip in the middle of the night? Why didn't she get in the Mustang he had wired? He could be back home cooking risotto alla Siciliana. She was pissing him off. Moron kid doesn't understand it ain't gonna do her no good. We're everywhere. We do business with almost two thirds of the fucking American population. We got the gambling, legal and non, a piece of the dog races, horse races, bingo, numbers, poker, team and individual betting on every sport or proposition from an election to who will be the next Miss America. Did the public think when they watch the pageant on TV, it was just the girls backstage that were getting fucked? We also got the loan-sharking, prostitution, labor racketeering and extortion. The legitimate real estate, shopping centers, every little fast food or pizza joint she could walk into would squeal on her if we let the word out. We got better coverage than the FBI and CIA put together.

He stepped out of the phone booth, checked his reflection on the dusty glass wall, smoothed his hair and straightened his tie. He had personally killed some of the toughest people in the country. He had come up in the fratellanza, now he was a gabellotto, a man of respect. Did this stupid kid think she could escape his hands?

Chapter 13

DEVLIN was the first one up. His first act was to call Frank. They were settled in at Nine 23rd Avenue. Dev told Holenka the phone number and demanded a promise that police cars would not patrol the house in any pattern that might draw attention. Frank agreed on condition that Dev stayed in constant contact. They had a deal.

Devlin slept in the living room instead of the second bedroom. It would be easier to hear a car pulling up in the driveway. He had bought the groceries yesterday at the ShopRite. The canned goods and the other non-perishables were still sitting in the bags, stacked up on the kitchen counter. The frozen food, meat and fish were already in the refrigerator. He had always been handy in the kitchen and a decade of bachelor life had improved it. He hoped he had gotten the right stuff.

For Sara, who said she was a vegetarian but didn't mind a dish of take-out chicken, he had gotten a few specialties. Cheese pizza, and being that she was his little girl, one packet of gummy bears and red licorice. Maggie's menu was a mystery. He did remember the imported King Oscar sardines, the seven grain bread, the cottage cheese, and the herbal tea. He had found Celestial Seasoning and chosen Red and Lemon Zinger.

For him it was simple. Soup. He grew up eating

Campbell's, the vegetable and tomato were the household specialties. Pop had insisted on it because his friend Ernie Fallon was the foreman of the Camden plant. Skippy Peanut Butter. He bought the creamy kind. Hope the kid doesn't go for the chunky. And Oreos, you never can go wrong with two packs.

Okay, they would be fed. More importantly, they must develop a routine that would keep them under cover for the next two weeks. Out of sight, out of mind, and out of harm's way. He brought cards. We'll teach the kid how to play gin. Or casino, three of us can play that together. Used to play that at the beach with the boys for a nickel a point in the old days. Monopoly. I brought the set. Can't grow up in this neighborhood and not play the game. Me and "The Fish" once had a running game for ten days. Mrs. Karp would scream at us to go outside in the sunshine and not stay locked up in his bedroom. Oh, yeh, water her geraniums.

Maggie opened the bedroom door. She wore Sara's T-shirt from Mainland High. Nothing else.

"Good morning, Dev."

He couldn't answer. Just smile, nod and admire. First thing in the morning, no make up, didn't need it, hair a bit tousled, and those legs that had hypnotized him at first sight eighteen years ago had not lost their shape. She had improved with age. No question, she was stunning. She headed for the one bathroom they all must share. He watched her cross the room, hoping the T-shirt would swirl and rise a bit. He stared at the door. In two seconds, it opened. Just her head appeared. Then an arm and one bare shoulder. She pointed to the linen closet.

"Would you please hand me two fresh towels. For my shower, and Sara's."

He leaped to his feet, took one step, and a half smile surfaced. "Wash your back?"

She pursed her lips and gave it mock serious thought. "Nah, we'll skip it today. But keep in touch."

She took the offered towels and slipped away. Dev ran his fingernails along the door and issued a low howl. He subdued the wolf and decided to set the breakfast table instead. He neatly prepared place settings for each, poured orange juice and put the bread in the toaster oven. He surveyed his handiwork. Milk. He had forgotten milk. Napkins. There were no napkins. He could use his sleeve, but not the Tyler woman. Sara should have some too. Let's raise her with class. None in the closet. Mister and Missus Karp, I can't believe this. How the hell could someone in the deli business not have paper goods ?

He tapped on the bathroom door. "Maggie."

"No, thank you, Dev. I already washed my back and I'm managing to dry myself off."

He was falling in love all over again. Maybe he had never fallen out. "I'm going to the Wawa around the corner to pick up milk and napkins. Do you want anything?"

"Yes, toothpaste. Crest or Aquafresh."

"I'll be back in ten minutes. Please tell Sara not to step out."

"Don't worry, you'll be lucky if she's out of the shower in thirty."

Dev waved a silent goodbye, knowing he couldn't be heard over the hair dryer. Living with these two females was going to be a new experience on many levels.

The Wawa convenience stores were well established in the South Jersey shore area, but competition from Seven Eleven was keen. Twenty-four hour service was becoming mandatory in many locations. Attracting good help for these schedules was always a problem. Saud Behan, the newly appointed manager of the Longport Wawa, greeted Devlin.

"Good morning, sir. What can I help you with, sir?"

Devlin nodded and checked the round name badge. "Toothpaste, Saud. And napkins."

"On aisle two, sir. Sid, I am called, Sid."

Devlin found the napkins and the toothpaste. Question is should he buy the munchies for himself now, or wait a day. He forgot the potato chips and the Frito Lays when he went to the ShopRite. Beer pretzels could wait till he was back at the Shamrock. Nah, let's show discipline, walk out of a Wawa for the first time in your life just buying what you came for. Besides, better not grow a gut in front of the girls. He brought his items to the checkout counter. "What's the damage?"

Saud totalled the purchase and smiled showing a glistening gold tooth. "You are new in the neighborhood. sir? I do not believe I have seen you before."

Devlin dropped a ten dollar bill. "Sid, what is this, twenty questions, or can I just get my groceries here?"

Saud bent his head in a half bow. "Oh, I beg your pardon, sir. No problem, no problem, sir. I was just trying to be neighborly."

He counted out the correct change in rapid movements and pushed it forward. Devlin picked up each coin slowly. Had he lost his cool over nothing? He smiled, gave Saud a two finger salute and sauntered out at an even pace. Saud smiled in response.

"Thank you for patronizing our store, sir. Please come again."

He watched Devlin exit, the golden tooth disappearing swiftly as the smile turned to a smoldering glare. Saud was quick to anger. These Americans are not respectful to the sons of Islam. He took pad and pen and watched the Volvo unhurriedly ease out of the parking lot. He wrote down the license plate numbers. A stranger in the neighborhood, one who objected to being called a stranger. Like Grey Eyes, he also had the instincts of a hunter. Unlike his position at the Wawa, his instincts were not newly acquired.

Saud Abdallah Behan was one of six brothers. The youngest, a member of the Islamic Jahid, had died last month, carrying a load of explosives attached to his body which exploded in a bus. Seven innocent civilians were also killed, but his family praised his martyr's death. More money and guns were needed. Saud would send his share from America.

If it meant sleeping with Mafia dogs, so be it.

After his call to Jamie, Grey Eyes returned to Berkley for one more look. The streets were empty, the neighbors either sleeping, doing housework or off to their jobs. He stopped in front of 59, walked around the back of the house, up the porch steps, peered in the windows, backtracked to the front door, rang the bell four times, returned to his car and waited fifteen minutes for a face to appear. No one showed. He telephoned the house from his car. No answer. Definitely she skipped.

He checked the camera. Four exposures left. Nikon, five hundred millimeter telephoto lens. Black and white film. He had already taken shots of the kid, the good looking blonde, who sure as shit is the kid's mother, Devlin and Holenka. He focused on the house, took three of 59, the windows and doors, one of 61, just the front door. That finished the roll. He made a gun with his forefinger and thumb, aimed it at the bedroom window over the garage. His tongue popped a small clicking sound against his bared teeth. A wolfish grin spread over his swarthy face as he drove around the corner to the pay phone on Shore Road.

His first call was to his client. He waited while the call was transferred. There was minor static, then a voice filtered through.

"Yeh, you finally got something for me."

This was the second time. Grey Eyes didn't like it. It was bad for his rep. "She skipped. I need some local help."

"I don't do that shit, that's why I hired you. You're supposed to be a fucking pro."

Grey Eyes rolled his head, took the crick out of his neck. "You want to get a new contractor? Say the word."

"No. Wait five minutes, then talk to Angelo. You got the number." The receiver slammed down.

He dialed the number. "Yeh, this is Angelo. Whattya need?"

"I need some pictures developed immediately. I want them spread around. Write these names down. Sara Johnson, Robert Devlin, Margaret Crandall. The first thing I wanna know is if they're trying to skip the country. Check everything, airports, private planes. Then check the trains, car rentals, everything else that moves that could relocate them from this area. Don't miss a fucking inch. Check three cars."

He snorted. "Make that two, one of 'em blew up. An '89 black Corvette, license number YLO 904, and a '90 dark green Volvo, license 436LLW. I wanna call if anyone of those cars is spotted. I'll be there in thirty minutes."

It was eleven-thirty when Sara finally strolled into the living room. Dev was watching a rerun of last year's Phoenix open on ESPN. He became interested in golf one summer when he worked at Atlantic City Country Club. He didn't caddy, he parked cars. He saw a few of the members hitting off the tee and decided it wasn't such a difficult game. He tried it and found out otherwise.

Maggie was writing in her journal. She had kept one for years and knew the next two weeks would provide memorable entries. She stopped to greet her daughter. "Good morning, Sara. Almost good afternoon. Have a good night's sleep?"

Sara yawned and nodded, unsure what to call Maggie. Mother didn't feel right. Surely not yet. She headed for the bathroom. Dev shrugged, Maggie smiled and called out, "There's a fresh towel for you behind the door."

At twelve-ten, Sara reappeared, freshly showered, her golden hair dried, settling softly on the shoulders of her Hard Rock Cafe T-shirt. Dev looked at his watch, and realized there would have to be a family discussion regarding the use of the facilities or he would turn into a camel. Sara drank her orange juice without sitting down and turned toward the bedroom. Maggie put down her journal.

"Is that all you're having for breakfast?"

"Hey, Mag, you sound like Mrs. Karp. Let the kid eat what she wants."

"I don't eat too much in the morning. Thanks for making the juice for me."

"Dev made breakfast for all of us."

Sara gave him a beaming smile that warmed his heart. He'd make four meals a day for this kid. "Thank *you*, Dev. Should I call you, Dev, or Bobby? Like Frank does."

He knew what he wanted her to call him. "Call me, sir. I'm kidding, I'm kidding. Dev is fine."

The phone's sudden ring startled them into silence. They remained motionless, frozen in the grip of it's threatening intrusion. Dev answered.

"Yes." He smiled and shook his head. "I want you to know, Frank, you scared the crap out of us. What's up?"

"Just checking. I know you have the station number, but in case of an emergency, write down my home number and the number of the car phone. You guys are all set to stay inside, right?"

"Only went to the Wawa on Shore Road for some milk, otherwise we are tucked in for the season."

"Don't go out again. I'll come over with a quart."

Sara raised her hand. "Trish used to buy it by the gallon, put it in quart containers and freeze it. That way we'll have enough for days."

Maggie waved to Dev. " Let me speak to him. Hello, Frank. My father doesn't know where we are. I left him a note. I told him that I wouldn't be available for the next two weeks. No, Frank, no. I didn't tell him where we might be going. You and Dev asked me not to, so I didn't."

"You're not going to tell your father?" asked Sara. That was her grandfather. Unseen, unknown, now uninformed.

Maggie saw the incredulous look on Sara's face. "Listen, Frank, he is my father, you can tell him anything about the business. You heard the will." She bit her lip in a flood of embarrassment, turned her head away from Sara's view and continued. "He knows nothing other than that I was trying to sell the land for two million."

Devlin couldn't hear Holenka's answer, but he knew how he would handle this. The old man wouldn't give the dust under his fingernail for Sara and probably wished the mick lifeguard had been the car bomb victim. He wouldn't tell him diddly squat.

"Alright, Frank. You will be the only that knows where we are. Yes, we will. Goodbye." She hung up. "He wants us to stay out of sight and under cover."

Devlin took his two women by the hand and with their arms over each other shoulders, their heads touching, they went into a huddle. There was a tension and an excitement. Their sweet smell surrounded him as he laughed quietly, catching them in its infection. He whispered the words, leaking them slowly into their closed tent of togetherness.

"Frank wants us to stay out of sight and under cover. He is one helluva smart cop. I thought that *was* the reason we knocked our brains out to come here."

Their arms held tighter as they rocked back and forth in nervous laughter.

Jonathan Bishop Crandall arrived home later than usual for a Wednesday. He had completed his customary routine of a morning round of golf, lunch with the other members of the foursome, two hours of bridge in the club cardroom, a martini in the bar, then his steam, massage, shower and shave. Skip, one of the attendants in the Men's locker room, had scratched one of Crandall's new Bally loafers. It had to be polished three times before Crandall approved of the appearance.

Margaret wasn't home. It was true he and Ellen hadn't spent that much time together, but he liked companionship. He had successfully found it elsewhere all his life. The red dot of the answering machine blinked rapidly. Only one message. Good. He hated intrusions on his plans. And he had exciting plans for this evening. The call was from Jessica Stanton. Three times in one week. Couldn't we get together for dinner? Holy Hannah, that woman is persistent. It's true she was Alfred's widow, he had been a good friend and a great stockbroker, but just because we both are "now alone," as she put it, I will not be maneuvered into winding up with her. Women still find me attractive enough to have my female company age forty, not sixty.

The note from Maggie was on the end table next to the answering machine. He read it, crumpled it and threw it to the floor. She's gone off with that mick lifeguard and his bastard daughter. Ellen had fawned over that damn infant so much, she had no right to complain if I found my solace elsewhere.

What is wrong with Margaret? Where is that girl's head. Now to get in touch with her, I have to call some cop. I thought I brought her up with more sense. We certainly gave her the best education money could buy and she disappears in the middle of the negotiations of an important property sale. She was asking two million. That could set me right again. Of course half is mine.

Chapter 14

MEDFORD had the contracts of sale prepared, along with a full set of closing documents. There would be no purpose to sign contract, put down a deposit and set a closing date for the future. There was no time. They must go directly to a close. The documents were set to be Federal Expressed to Devlin's office, as the damned two-bit operator had demanded, but the price of twenty million had not been inserted. Zeist had not yet agreed and, for a certainty, Trentino never would. There was another problem. Devlin was now impossible to contact. All calls to his office had remained unreturned. How dare this nobody ignore him! Zeist called daily, demanding progress.

"Addison, you know I'm a patient man. I am, however, running out of time to put up with your dalliances." Zeist stroked his moustache with ever increasing rapidity, attempting to calm himself down. Don't blow up; you still need this idiot to close the deal. "Give me a firm date when I can assure the lenders we will have clear title. We're coming down to the wire."

Throughout his career, Medford had never felt so hemmed in. So helpless. His voice was pleading. Zeist almost didn't recognize it. "Max, the Crandall woman and this Devlin have disappeared from the face of the earth. I've prepared all the documents except, of course, for the price that you haven't given me final approval on. Max, if they don't show, or we don't get signatures, there will be no closing."

Zeist removed his fingers from his moustache and pursed his lips thoughtfully. Disappeared from the face of the earth. Did Little Vinnie do me a good deed? "What do you mean they disappeared? Have there been any police or news reports on their whereabouts?"

"Sorry, Max, no reports. I know what you're thinking. Undoubtedly they're alive and well. I just don't know where. Should I fill in the price of twenty million and Fed Ex it to Devlin's office?"

The Max kept a gold Asian coin on his desk. It was a souvenir of his first trip to the Orient. He flipped it. It landed heads. "Addison, let me ask you a question. Will Great Eastern give us a title policy if we show them a contract signed by all parties of interest, even though we haven't closed yet?"

"I would say, probably, yes. Of course, they will take twenty million out of the financing proceeds and keep it in escrow until you do close title on that sliver."

Zeist rubbed the gold coin with his forefinger. "That's very interesting. Let me see if I've got this straight. If something happens to the girl before she becomes of age, I inherit that sliver for nothing, and a closing isn't necessary. If she is around to collect, we pay the twenty million and close. In all events, with a signed contract, I control the damn sliver. Correct?"

"Correct."

"Then either way, I can close my financing?"

"Correct again."

Zeist picked up the gold coin and kissed it. "Fill in the price of twenty million and get the damn thing signed."

The windows of the Atlantic Avenue, Longport Wawa, like all the others in the chain, were plastered with signs signifying specials and services. During the summer months, soda, salads, subs and picnic supplies received the best display. Year-round, a small yellow sign with black lettering offering FAX, $1.25, remained visible in the corner of the main window.

Saud heard the click and the whine of an incoming message. The faces of Sara, Maggie and Devlin poured out in grainy black and white. The features were clear and easily identifiable. Following was a sheet of information and instructions, ending with a phone number and the name, Angelo.

The gold tooth glared in a wide grin as Saud picked up Devlin's picture first. He lay the picture on the deli counter, brought the sharp cheese knife to the corners and trimmed it. He leaned close to the face.

"You should be friendlier to your neighbors, Mr. Robert Devlin. It is certain you must be my neighbor. Nobody drives more than two miles for milk. That is the custom in your country. And that is surely a certainty in Longport, USA, my disrespectful customer."

He dialed Angelo. Grey Eyes was right. His people were everywhere.

Jonathan waited a day before he called Holenka and two days before he returned Jessica Stanton's call. She had been his wife's best friend, even though it was obvious to him that she preferred his company. On the occasions Jessica had overdone her white wine spritzer intake, she had thrown caution to the winds and herself at Jonathan. The Stanton's daughter, Vivien, was a girlhood friend of Margaret's, an alliance that strengthened when the young girls were classmates at Pilgrim Academy. Though Vivien lived nearby in Longport, he never saw her. Jessica was the one he had to deal with. It would be foolish to ignore her. She spends like a drunken sailor, but it would take her a hundred years to go through all the money Alfred left her.

There should still be a bundle left in case all his other plans didn't work out and he decided to marry her. Lord knows, he preferred his women twenty years younger, but she wasn't bad looking and he had known her for thirty years. There wouldn't be any surprises. He could still come and go as he pleased. There was no rush, she'd never turn him down.

Jonathan Bishop Crandall had spent his entire life never being turned down. His parents, Victoria and Edward Crandall, were an old main line Philadelphia family that lived in luxury and raised their children accordingly. His mother had trouble conceiving her first two children. When they were born, after difficult pregnancies, she hoped that was the last of her progeny and pain. That was not to be. Both were girls. Edward insisted on a male heir to carry on the family name.

Jonathan arrived four years after his sister, Charlotte. His long awaited arrival, combined with his exceptional good looks, made him the center of a predominately female household. There was no indulgence that Edward, his mother or his sisters did not allow the boy. He was also named after his Grandmother Bishop, another source of gifts and praise. As a child of ten, he was the young girl's prize at dancing class. At seventeen, an eighteen-year-old from Vassar was attracted to his assured manner, blonde wavy hair, square jaw and dazzling smile that lit up his perpetually tanned face. A female older than himself. This was quite a coup, but just another step. Women were, and would be, attracted to him all his life.

When the Crandalls summered in Atlantic City, their three children, Beth, Charlotte and Jonathan, mingled with the prominent local families. Ellen Tyler, sheltered, wealthy and shy, was a plum that easily fell into young Jonathan's lap. At twenty-two he well understood the importance of marrying wealth. And she was an only child of an aged father. He kept Ellen on a tight string, but continued to play the field, a practice he would resume during their marriage. In those years, in his class, husbands rarely beat their wealthy wives. They abused them in other ways. By control.

In return for allowing Margaret to give birth to Devlin's bastard child, Ellen had signed power-of-attorney and conceded full financial control to her husband. Jonathan's supervision of the Tyler wealth had not been too successful. He had lost heavily in commodities in orange futures. In 1993 he was going to recoup in a major stock market trade. His stockbroker, a partner at Stanton and Blenders, his friend Alfred's old firm, told him about Synergen, a biotech company. The company had developed Antril, a drug claiming to sharply reduce septic shock during an operation. The stock had been as low as 8, was now up to 23, and, after FDA approval, could go to a 100. Jonathan wanted the big hit, but decided to wait till Monday. Over the weekend, he spoke to friends from the country club. Two were in Synergen up to their necks. This was the hot one.

He hadn't slept home Sunday night. Happily occupied elsewhere, he didn't call his broker till ten. Synergen was up to 29½ bid, 31, asked. He liquidated everything in every account and bought Synergen at the market. When it hit 53, he put in a sell order for 55. It closed the day at 54. The boys at the club said it was going to 100, maybe 125. He canceled the sell order, doubled the family holdings, borrowing the full allowable amount on margin. The interest costs would be pennies compared to the millions he would wrap up.

Two days later the stock reached 65. Before the day was over, the FDA announced that the phase three trials showed the study of the drug to be not effective. Trading in Synergen was halted. When it reopened, it was down thirty points within the hour. Crandall's margin borrowings were called and his entire equity was wiped out. The major hit turned out to be a major disaster. Ellen died within six months, never knowing how her estate had been decimated.

Crandall's call to Holenka had lifted his spirits. There was twenty million on the table, not just two. If I got my fair share, I could be back in the game again. There had to be some way it didn't all go to the mongrel brat. I know I could convince Margaret, if that damn cop would tell me where they are. He called Holenka back.

"Holenka."

"Sergeant, this is Mr. Crandall again."

"It's Captain. What can I do for you?"

"It's important that I speak to my daughter, and I must have the phone number."

"I told you before, Mr. Crandall, I can't give you the number, but give me any message you want and I'll deliver it."

Crandall slapped his thigh in frustration. "You can tell Margaret that she is being incredibly irresponsible. There is a land sale here involving a great deal of money and, in her absence, I should be handling it."

"Her first, and most important, responsibility is to protect her daughter's life. Aren't you concerned about your own daughter's life?"

"I certainly am, but that is not. . . ."

"I'll give her your message."

Holenka hung up leaving Crandall fuming at the dead phone in his hand which he proceeded to slam down. It settled into its cradle and rang. Crandall snatched it up.

"You've got some nerve hanging up on me, I'll speak to your superiors about you. To the mayor. I am not without connections in this community."

Before Crandall could take his turn at hanging up, an unknown voice spoke.

"Is this the Crandall residence ?"

He was chagrined. "Yes."

"This is Betty Walsh. I'm Addison Medford's secretary. If you have a moment, he'd like to speak with you."

Medford, the lawyer on the land deal. Not that boorish cop. This was more like it.

"Yes, Mr. Medford, so glad you called, I was just about to ring you."

"How do you do, Mr. Crandall. Were you going to

call me with some news of your daughter's whereabouts? I've not been able to contact her. Or Bob Devlin."

Crandall clenched his jaw at the mention of Devlin's name. "No, I'm sorry Mr. Medford, I don't know where they are at present, but if you would like to discuss the matter of the land sale, I can handle it. Family financial matters are left up to me."

"I don't know if this is typical of your area of responsibility, Mr. Crandall. This also involves Sara Johnson's interests."

Crandall swallowed the gall rising in his chest. This brat! This bastard offspring of his would be the same bane that her low-class Irish father was. He cleared his throat. "I am the child's grandfather."

He surprised himself. How easily it came out. "Perhaps we should meet to review in what way we can go forward with the matter."

Medford was annoyed, pressed for time as he had never been before, and now this old man wanted to be a player. Was he a source of information ? He asked again. "Do you know where they are ?"

"No, but I can easily find out."

Medford was an astute listener. Crandall had emphasized the word easily. "Time is vital. We're attempting to tie this in with another closing."

Crandall admired himself in the hall mirror. He needs it for another closing. Opportune time for the squeeze play. "I'm quite confident I can supply you with what you need. Perhaps, if I can accommodate you with a prompt response, you could accommodate me with a small advance on the selling price. By coincidence, I'm also planning another closing. You know how funds get held up."

Medford smiled for the first time in days. His funds are held up. He means lost. Medford had seen copies of Crandall's trade slips on Synergen, which were on file at Franklin Trust, as security for loans. Courtesy of Rickic Murdock. Crandall had purchased two hundred thousand shares at an average of thirty-one, for a total cost of six million, two hundred thousand. It all had been lost, every cent, when the margin calls wiped him out.

"Perhaps we can, Mr. Crandall. Could you come to my office tomorrow?"

"What time?"

"Two. I'm in the Packard Building. Ms.Walsh will tell you where to park. See you then, Mr. Crandall."

"I'll be there."

The first two days of togetherness, under cover, were like the beginning of most relationships. Tenuous. Finding one's territory, the parameters of what to say, how to say it, what to do, and how to do it. Maggie and Dev's memories of their past had been partially lost in the haze of time. The space was also limited. The curtains on the front windows were drawn and the only natural light came in from the sides or the back porch sliding doors. It became a big deal to put your head outdoors to get fresh air or sunshine. They played odd finger wins to see which one went out back to water Mrs. Karp's geraniums.

Most of the houses had been closed now that the summer season was over. The only action on their street was the traffic coming and going to the volunteer fire department across the street. Dev had prepared for this isolation with a good supply of games. Cards. He would teach Sara how to play hearts. If she knew casino, the three of them could enjoy that. Before this siege would be over, she'd never forget the good ten, the good two, or how to win cards and spades. Maggie hated gin rummy. She preferred bridge.

Being a native of AC environs, he had grown up playing Monopoly. He brought the set he had since he was nine. The box had been opened and closed so many times, the P had worn out and now read, arker Brothers. Ironic. On this very same board, Lennie Karp had owned Illinois and Indiana when he owned Marvin Gardens and Ventnor. He offered to trade Kentucky for Atlantic. Lennie would have the reds, and he would have the yellows. They negotiated for three days and no deal. He brought an extra pair of dice to teach Sara the thrill of the crap table. What the hell, if they collected twenty million, they could splurge with a thousand. The highlight was waiting for Frank's call, to get news from the outside. He was coming over tomorrow night at eight. There were items he wanted to discuss in person. He was also bringing the milk.

Saud had seen people die many times. In the village where he had grown up, life was cheap. He was not easily frightened. When Grey Eyes took him to the back room, Saud recognized the smell of death this man carried. Grey Eyes surveyed Devlin's picture and the number of the license plate of the Volvo.

"This is the man, sir. He came into the store two days ago driving a green car with this number. He has not returned."

Grey Eyes fingered the sharply cut edge of Devlin's picture. His face was expressionless. "You told Angelo you think he's from the neighborhood."

"He bought milk, sir." The gold tooth was displayed in the triumphant smile proclaiming his shrewdness.

The killer barely nodded. "Did you watch him when he pulled out of the parking lot?"

"Oh, yes, sir. I watched closely. Very closely. He turned to the left, which is the south. That is not the direction to the Longport Boulevard bridge, or to Atlantic City. That is towards the dead end part of the island. To the Point. There is no way out." The dark brown eyes sparkled with pride.

Smart little gook. "Gimme a map of this part of the island." Saud deftly picked a map off the rack and traced the area with his finger, from 26th Avenue to the Point.

"Call me in the car if you see anything else. Here's the number. Don't fuck up."

Saud stiffened in his heart, but the smile remained on his face. There was no need for him to be disrespectful to me. I have been a loyal soldier. This one also does not understand the people of Islam.

Grey Eyes got into his car, opened the map again. Not too bad. At least they were cornered in a box, down to the Point. Five-thirty. He started to cruise the blocks.

Chapter 15

GREY Eyes started his search from 26th Avenue, heading south to the Point. Most of the houses, while not occupied by year-rounders, were still used for weekends through the fall. He drove slowly, ignoring those with shuttered windows, his monotone voice speaking softly into a recorder, methodically transcribing which blocks had been covered, and noting which houses warranted a revisit. He continued cruising for two and a half hours without stopping and covered his defined area three times. He checked his watch, did one more run, at a faster pace, finishing up at the Point.

He parked on Atlantic Avenue, took the tape recorder and the food he had brought from the Wawa; a hard roll, an apple, a wedge of provolone and iced tea. He sat on a bench facing the bay side of the Point, ate, listened to the tape and attracted the gulls with half of his uneaten roll. The gulls approached warily, their sharp, beady eyes watching his sudden moves, as he tossed the crumbs. The black shiny orbs staring at him brought back memories of Brooklyn and his practice of shooting gulls with his twenty-two. He was the only one of his gumbahs that could hit a bird, dead center in the eye, without marking the head. The tape finished playing. He would cruise two more times while there was still daylight, then return tonight to see which houses showed lights on at night.

Jonathan Crandall was not a punctual man. He didn't have to be. All of his life people had waited for him. This was a day to be on time. He was at the receptionist desk of Stern, Bradford and Altschuler at one fifty-five, for an appointment at two. A record for him. He was announced, advised that someone would be out shortly to show him to Mr. Medford's office. He nodded and flashed a dazzling smile. It always paid to have receptionists be responsive. Many of them, along with private secretaries, had extended him business courtesies along with their personal favors. He straightened his Hermes tie under the double breasted navy blue blazer with its AC country club emblem, smoothed the hair at his temples and was prepared for his entrance. Last week someone had said he looked like Joseph Cotten. In that Orson Welles movie. It was always on the old movie channel.

Ms. Walsh came for him. She controlled her astonishment at his appearance. Medford had told her it was Margaret Tyler Crandall's father. If it was, he had aged incredibly well. It was impossible to ignore his mature good looks. They exchanged admiring glances. She extended her hand. He took it and held it.

"How do you do, Mr. Crandall. I'm Mr. Medford's secretary, Betty Walsh." She slowly removed her hand from his. "If you'll come this way, Mr. Medford is expecting you."

Crandall walked behind her, not alongside. He admired her shapely legs that tapered down to perfectly molded slim ankles, her high heel shoes, with satin laces neatly tied. Her full hips surrounded a body that appealed to him as he watched each movement, each twitch, with each step. It would be a pleasure to stay in touch. They arrived at Medford's office. She held the door for him, leaving a minuscule bridge between their bodies as he brushed her.

"If there is anything I can do for you, don't hesitate to call."

He smiled. No, he wouldn't hesitate. He never did. Medford rose from his desk to greet him.

"Thank you for coming, Mr. Crandall."

"It's my pleasure. Jonathan, please call me Jonathan." He settled himself in the chair to which Medford pointed, unbuttoned his blazer, scanned the room, inwardly nodding his appreciation of the surroundings. "I understand the price has been settled."

"Oh, yes. The price has been agreed upon. Twenty million. Not an insignificant sum and a very generous offer on the part of my client. I imagine your family is quite happy about that."

Crandall rubbed his hands and basked in the warmth of big business. "Good, good. Yes, I'm sure that will please my family. When do you anticipate the closing to take place?"

"That's hard to say. The contracts and the related closing documents were Federal Expressed to Mr. Devlin's office last night and should have arrived this morning. Do you know Mr. Devlin ?"

Crandall responded with a dour smile and a curt nod.

Medford noted Crandall's expression. Good. A discriminating ally. "I couldn't hazard a guess as to the closing date. We still have nothing signed, by either party."

Jonathan sighed in frustration. The Buyer hasn't signed. How could Margaret leave in the middle of this?

Medford continued. "Our problem here is one of time. I mentioned that to you on the phone. We need to get the parties together, or at least let me know where your daughter is so we can explain our timetable. I was hoping you could help us in that regard."

Crandall rose, ceremoniously buttoned his blazer, and cleared his throat. "I generally do take care of family matters, most of them are entrusted to me. My latc wife depended on me and my daughter, and now, of course, my granddaughter's affairs have my full and devoted attention. Unfortunately, I don't know where they are at present."

He smoothed his tie, shook his head, and smiled at Medford, knowing the attorney, even though he was about the same age as his daughter, could sympathize with his plight. "You know how you youngsters are. Go off on a little jaunt to do your thing and never tell us old folks of your whereabouts." He finished with a small chuckle, again displaying his attractive smile.

Medford also stood, his slight frame a shadow of Crandall's imposing figure. He smiled in return. Maybe this blowhard knows something. "You mentioned an advance. It would be difficult to satisfy your request on a contract that hasn't even been signed. I'm sure you can appreciate the merit of that."

"Of course, of course."

"What would be helpful, Mr. Crandall - Jonathan - if I may repeat, is to let us know where they are. We can contact them and conclude the matter." Medford stepped toward the door, indicating the meeting was over. "That's about all we can do at this juncture. Thank you very much for coming in."

Crandall shook Medford's outstretched hand, started for the door and stopped. "If I could locate them for you, I'm not saying I can, but if I could, on a twenty million dollar deal, an advance of only five percent seems reasonable. Don't you think so?"

"That's a million. I'd say that's a rather substantial sum on a matter that hadn't closed yet."

"How about a quarter of a million?"

Medford smiled. The old fish was biting. At least he'd go to work. "I'm sure we can work something out. The important thing is to locate them. Thank you again for coming. Goodbye, Jonathan."

He ushered Crandall toward Ms. Walsh's desk and disappeared into his office. Crandall waved farewell to Ms. Walsh and was about to depart when she rose from behind her desk and accompanied him to the reception area. This time they walked side by side, Ms. Walsh's eyes fastened to his, ignoring the envious glances of her female co-workers.

Medford's FedEx package arrived at Devlin's office at ten. Grace signed for it and put it on Tess's desk. With the due date for her baby only three weeks away, Tess spent a lot of time in the bathroom. She returned to her desk, ready to do battle. Whenever Devlin was out of the office for more than a day, Tess opened his mail and took his phone calls. She knew his present absence would be for an indeterminate period. Devlin had left her specific instructions, neatly typed out.

Dear Little Mother,

1. The only way you can contact me is through Frank Holenka. His numbers, office and home, are on my Roladex.

*2. Our phone may be tapped. When you call Frank, block a trace with *67.*

3. When, or I should say, if, the sale documents come in from Medford, hand deliver a set to Albert Levy. He's the lawyer who's going to represent the Seller. Enclose a note, tell him not to do his usual nit picking delay. He always drags. Thinks his fee will be bigger. We don't care about a few thousand on adjustments, we just want to close A.S.A.P.

4. Call Frank, and ask him to bring me a full set of the documents for review and signature after we get Levy's comments.

5. Hold your water till October 9th.

Luvya, Dev

Tess opened the FedEx package and separated the documents into three sets. One for her office file, one for Holenka and one for Darlene, who would deliver it to Levy's office. Darlene could leave early; it would be on her way to Friday's, just up the road.

The choice of Albert Levy for the Seller's lawyer, had been discussed by Sara, Maggie and Devlin before the move to Longport. The women had left the decision to him. That knowledge would have sent Jonathan Bishop Crandall into a fuming rage. The Irish lifeguard, not he, was handling the family finances.

Holenka had just completed his review of the car bomb file when Tess called. Yes, he could pick up Devlin's real estate papers and deliver them this afternoon. He wanted to speak to Sara again about her recollection of the man she saw in the mall. The file already contained information from the Federal Bureau of Alcohol, Tobacco and Firearms. They had supplied him with a list of individuals, and their photos; known to have used a car bomb device. Sara had provided the police artist with some description and sketches had been made.

He called the Longport number. Maggie answered. Holenka said he would be there this afternoon instead of tonight. He was bringing the contracts from Medford. Tell Sara he was also bringing an Identa Kit. An interesting police tool. A series of facial features on a clear plastic background that overlayed one on the other to form a face. They would play a game of matching one up. Maggie approved. Sara is bored and will enjoy the distraction.

In a few short days Sara had developed a case of cabin fever. Being pent up, without companionship her own age, exercise or fresh air was contrary her teenage spirit and buoyant nature. She checked the clock in the kitchen. Three fifteen. Working with Frank would be a diversion. He said he would be there at four. Another forty-five minutes. She flopped down on the couch with her dog-eared copy of *Catcher In The Rye*.

3:50. Holenka was heading south on Atlantic Avenue.

3:55. Grey Eyes was heading north on Atlantic Avenue, got off at 26th to recheck one house. Nothing. Back to Atlantic.

Holenka had brought Devlin's package of documents, the Identa Kit and part of the car bomb file. There were six photos he wanted Sara to study. He slowed down to make the left turn onto 23rd. The volunteer firemen were taking the hook and ladder out for a drill. He stopped and waited till they pulled past him. From behind the long, swinging hook and ladder truck, Grey Eyes watched. He saw Holenka. He looked at the four photos on the seat next to him. The cop. Holenka proceeded down 23rd. Grey Eyes didn't follow. He could come back in three minutes and see which house the cop parked in front of. It didn't matter which one, there were only eight houses. Now he knew the block. What he didn't know was that Holenka had also seen him.

Holenka pulled past number nine and parked in front of the house across the street. He slid down in the seat, out of sight, and adjusted the mirror at an angle that allowed him to see anyone approaching from the rear. He removed his Smith and Wesson nine millimeter hand gun from its holster and placed it on the passenger seat. Then he called the Longport police. He spoke softly and firmly.

"This is Captain Holenka of AC detectives. I'm staked out in a blue Chevy on 23rd just past the fire house. There is a strong possibility that the guy who did the car bomb job in Linwood will be coming by here. Bring me some back-up. In unmarked cars. No sirens, no noise. The suspect is in a black Buick BAH 440." They acknowledged and signed off. Holenka wiped the sweat off his upper lip and waited.

4:07. Devlin was exercising on the bedroom floor. Maggie was writing in her journal. Sara had put her book down and was impatiently flicking the TV remote from Oprah to QVC. She turned off the TV, circled the room, finishing at the front window. She peeked through the curtains. When was Frank coming? Let's do something already. Hey, that's Frank's car across the street. Why doesn't he come in? I'll bet he's napping. Do cops always nap in the car?

Frank wasn't napping. He was watching the progress of the black Buick that had entered 23rd. It stopped. Holenka picked up the Smith and Wesson and released the safety. Two more cars turned into 23rd. The man in the Buick spun around and watched them. When they pulled into the firehouse, he redirected his attention to the house next to Holenka's car.

4:10. Sara opened the curtains further. That was definitely Frank's car. "Maggie, Frank's out front."

Maggie was deeply involved in her writing. "Hm, good."

Sara opened the front door. "I'm going to get some fresh air and walk Frank in."

Devlin, resting between sit-ups, heard her. He called quickly. "Sara, stay inside!"

She opened the front door and stepped onto the porch as Devlin leaped to his feet. The next minute was a blur of explosions that shattered the calm seashore street.

Grey Eyes was out of his car in seconds, an Uzi aimed at Sara. Holenka fired two shots. Devlin sprung through the door, tackling Sara to the porch deck. Three rapid bursts flew past them, hitting the side of the house. The two police cars sped into the street, guns blazing at Grey Eyes, who blasted his Uzi in return. Holenka's third shot caught Grey Eyes in the neck, the policemen in the front car riddled Grey Eyes with a fusillade. He fell to the curb. The driver of the front police car lay slumped on the steering wheel. A bullet from the Uzi, had passed through his eye, out the back of his head.

Devlin picked up his daughter, brushed her bruised knees and attempted to calm her hysteria. He led her into the house and Maggie's arms. He went back outside to meet Frank and view the carnage. They stood on the curb as the body of Grey Eyes was turned over.

The Longport policemen hovered over their fallen comrade. Holenka and Devlin offered their sympathies. Holenka requested a twenty-four police guard on the house till they vacated and no media report. There would have to be silence on this until Sara was totally safe. She wouldn't be for another ten days.

Chapter 16

IT had been a difficult night. At two-thirty Sara had awakened screaming. Maggie rushed in to comfort her as Devlin paced the living room, peering out with regularity at the police car stationed in front of the house.

"They're going to kill me, I know it." The tears streamed down her face, her hair matted from the dampened pillow. "I hope I wind up in heaven. At least I'll see Trish and Alex."

Her breast heaved with sobs and her body trembled in Maggie's arms. They remained that way, mother and daughter, for what seemed an eternity. Her fears and tears seemed unending. Finally, Maggie lay the girl's weary head on the pillow and watched her fall asleep. It was three thirty. All three were sitting at the kitchen table at six when Frank arrived.

Frank had brought donuts for them and coffee in a container for himself. The orange juice on the table remained untouched. They sat in silence as Frank opened the car bomb folder. He took out a photo and put it in front of Sara's swollen red eyes.

"I'm just going to ask you to take a quick look. Is this the man you saw at the mall."

Sara picked up the photo. It wavered in her trembling fingers. She brushed the hair from her eyes, bit her lip, started to answer, but no voice was audible. She nodded. Frank reached for the photo. Sara held it tight. She swallowed hard and spoke in a whisper.

"Who was he?" she asked.

Frank eased the photo out of her hand. "Do you really want to know?"

She nodded again and again and again. Yes, she wanted to know. Who was this man who had killed all that was precious to her and also wanted her life? Frank stepped back to gain some distance.

"His name is Anthony Barbieri. Better known as 'Tony, The Barber.' A professional killer who is a suspect in over twenty murders. No definite information on where he's from, but the Feds think he operated out of the Midwest. Probably Chicago or Detroit. He is also a car bomb expert."

Devlin leaned over and gently rubbed Sara's arm. He clapped his hands in an air of finality. "Okay, now it's over. He's gone, you're safe. We're all safe. All we gotta do is just lay low for another week and we're home free."

"What is the *matter* with you, Bobby ? You think this hood just fell from the sky and landed on your block? I just told you who he is and where he's from. He didn't come from Chicago or Detroit to Atlantic City to walk on the boardwalk. When we had our discussions, we figured it's not Zeist. We figured it's Trentino's work. This guy was here by invitation. You think this is over? It ain't over till the fat lady sings and she ain't even started humming."

Maggie drove a hard stare at Devlin. "What's he talking about?"

"Hey, Bobby, didn't you tell her?"

Devlin jumped up, knocking his chair over. Sara pulled her hands from the table in panic. Devlin walked around the table slowly, calming his own tension and temper. He stroked Sara's hair as he passed her.

"No, Frank, I didn't tell her. I didn't think there was any point in scaring them any more than they are now.

Listen to me, all of you. This Barbieri is gone, it's what I said before. We've just got to find a place and lay low for another week."

Maggie's voice was hard and flat. "Thank you, Dev. Thank you for not telling me. For taking all these matters in your own hand and being so responsible. Is that why you never called me during all those years? Remaining responsible?"

Devlin dug his nails into his palm. "We'll talk about that some other time. All I said now was, let's find a place to keep Sara safe."

"You repeated that twice already," Maggie, said. "It was your idea to run from the house on Berkley. They found us here. They'll find us anywhere."

"What she's saying is not off the wall, Bobby. Why don't you do what I said in the first place. Stay at a motel with around-the-clock police protection. Or, better yet, come to the station house. Nobody is going to break in there."

"Frank, I told you before, my kid is not going to be in any jail." He saw Maggie's expressionless face. "Okay, okay, okay. I'm not deciding by myself. We're a family. We'll vote on it."

Sara put up both her hands, defending the onslaught. "Please, please, don't let them put me in a jail."

Maggie stood behind Sara's chair, leaned over, put her cheek next to her daughter's and wrapped her arms around the unhappy girl. "Don't worry, you won't have to go any place that will cause you any more unhappiness. There *is* another place we can go. My friend Vivien Stanton lives close by. On 13th Avenue. Only ten blocks away. She's in England with her husband."

Devlin furrowed his brow. "Vivien Stanton. Do I know her ? That name sounds so familiar."

"I don't think you met her, but you probably heard me mention her name. We went to Pilgrim Academy together. Her family and my family were old friends. They lived in Ventnor on Parkway. When Viv and I were ten, the two families took us to Europe on the Queen Elizabeth."

Sara's face had softened. She was learning about her mother. "Was she your best friend ?"

Maggie nodded. "She was and she still is. Wait until she finds out about you. Viv and Ken are going to be in London for six weeks. He's opening a branch for Stanton and Blender. Viv told me to use the house if I wanted some time away from Jonathan."

Sara smiled for the first time since the news of Tony the Barber. "She calls your father Jonathan?"

"Yes. My father liked all the young girls to call him by his first name. We can get into the house. I know the combination of the front door lock and alarm. Four, seventeen fifty-eight. Viv's birthday."

Devlin clapped again. "Great. We stay there for the week. I love it. Ten blocks away. Trentino will never figure we made a close move like that. What a great switch."

Frank threw up his hands in frustration. "What am I supposed to do, arrest you people and drag you off for your own good?"

The three stood, bunched together in solidarity. Frank surrendered in defeat. "Forget it. Do what you want, but I insist on checking out the security system and notifying the police of the switch. I want them there in two seconds if the alarm goes off."

"I think you're going to like what you see, Frank," said Maggie. "Viv and Ken have some very valuable artwork and they have a double security setup. The one on the roof goes off if any window is broken and it's easily heard at the police station, which is close by."

Frank closed his folder. "We'll see. Give me the address. You're not going anywhere until it's dark. That will give me time to check it after I stop at the police station. I want to make a call on the family of the young officer that got it. He took a lot of heat off of me during the . . . ."

They all were silent, in remembrance of the violent event. Devlin spoke for his family. "Frank, I. . .we, want to thank you for being out there for us."

"Bobby, you're like one of my own." He waved his hand closing the conversation. Then he smiled and added, "If I got hurt, you would have had to drag Danny down here to give me last rites. Okay, enough. What's the final decision? You coming with me or going to 13th Avenue?"

Sara put her hand on Devlin's. "You saved my life yesterday, Dev. My vote is to go."

Devlin nodded in agreement. Maggie shrugged. "Might as well make it unanimous. Viv is at The Savoy in London. I'll call and let her know we're staying here. At least we won't have to water Mrs. Karp's geraniums."

Medford and Zeist had many items to review on a daily basis, but the sliver was now always the first topic of conversation. "I'm happy to tell you, Max, we finally have movement. Devlin turned the contract over to some local nobody lawyer named Levy. A single practitioner. So far his comments have been minimal. We should have final agreement by tomorrow. I told him the form must be acceptable to Great Eastern Title. With any luck, I'll have it all approved with the title insurance guarantee the lender wants in forty-eight hours. As you know, it's customary for the buyer to sign first and Levy stands on piddling small, ceremony. It's nothing, let's give him what he wants. Do you need the entire contract?"

Zeist twirled the gold coin and patted it fondly when it came up heads. Heads was always lucky for him. It meant green light. Go. The pieces are all falling into place. "Good, good, Addison. As soon as it's ready, just fax me the signature page. I'll sign it, and you can send me the fully completed set as soon as possible. I spoke to Radcliff this morning. Excellent reports on the Casino Bond Referendum. The polls are showing a seventy-two percent approval. Oh, Addison, on the contract. The closing date?"

Medford placed the white queen in a checkmate position against the black king and smiled triumphantly. "I thought you might want to know that our requested closing date has not been objected to by Levy. October ninth. One day after her birthday. I'll call you tomorrow."

Jonathan Crandall was meticulous about the phone calls he returned. He only responded to those that fulfilled his needs. Just as he only heard the words to questions he asked. The first phone call he returned was to Penny Linden, a lovely blonde Continental Airline stewardess of Swedish background who flew out of Philadelphia. They had met last year when Jonathan was returning from Florida. Ellen's illness had kept her in New Jersey. Airline stewardesses are always attentive to their first class customers. Sometimes more so to the attractive male passengers. She picked up on the third ring. He would have waited for six.

"Hello." Her voice was breathless and melodic.

"Penny, this is Jonathan. You sound like you're panting. Are you so anxious to see me?"

She laughed lightly. "I'm always anxious to see you, but I'm puffing because you caught me just getting out of the shower."

"What are you wearing?"

"Your favorite outfit. And a wet towel."

He pictured the full breasts overflowing onto him. "I can't wait till tomorrow night. It's been a month. Where would you like to go for dinner? Do you want to go back to Le Bec Fin ?"

"I loved it and I'd love to spend the evening with you, but I can't. We're flying out of Newark in an hour and we'll be in Atlanta for the night. Sorry, darling, but gotta cancel. Will you give me a rain check?"

"I will give you a rain check till eternity."

They exchanged telephone kisses. No plans for tomorrow night. He hated cating alone. Especially at the club. He called Jessica Stanton. A good night to touch all the bases. She answered on the first ring, undoubtedly waiting for anyone to rescue her from her own boring company. Oh, God, she's clearing her throat. She did it twice before he heard her voice rise into what she must have thought was a musical note, one that irritated him endlessly.

"Hellooooh."

He responded to this absurd opera in kind.

"Jessicaaaa, it's Jonathan. I was thinking of you. It's been too long since we spent an evening together. Are you free for dinner tomorrow night ?"

"Oh, Jonathan, what a lovely surprise. I'd love it."

"Good. I know you don't like to eat late, so why don't we do the buffet at the club. I'll be playing golf in the afternoon, would you mind if I met you there? Upstairs, in the bar, six-thirty?"

"I look forward to it. I'll be waaaaiting."

He was teeing off at two, would have to shower, steam and have his massage. Yes. She unquestionably would be waiting.

Karl drove the big car, the seven passenger limo that Little Vinnie used only for special occasions. His visitors from Detroit had returned. Charlie Baldanno, along with his two hoods, Sal, a hulking Italian, and a short albino named Needles with piercing blue eyes that promised terror. Neither was as big as Karlufsky, but both were smarter. They went from the airport to Vinnie's favorite restaurant in South Philly to remove the taste of airline food.

Vinnie was Neapolitano and urged them to try the pasta Puttanesca. Testa di puorco was the house specialty, a healthy serving for six. A pig's head boiled with celery, carrots and onions. Three bottles of Livio Felluga merlot were downed quickly with the meal. Baldanno gave the repast a nod, but proclaimed the food at Greektown in Detroit to be better. No business was discussed. That was being saved for the meeting which would come later, uninterrupted, behind the laundry at Brandywine Linen Services.

The room was small, poorly lit, with only a single fluorescent fixture at the door and a bulb on a cord that hung over the scarred dinette table isolated in the center of the cement floor. The noise from the laundry would give any recording device substantial interference. Charlie sat at one end of the table, pointed to the other for Vinnie. Sal and Needles stood behind Charlie. Baldanno's five foot six frame, formerly covered with muscle now turned to two hundred and ten pounds of fat, overwhelmed the small kitchen table. He patted his stomach and belched. "Too fuckin' much garlic in the escarole. You got something to drink."

Karl went to the small refrigerator in the corner and held up a Diet Pepsi. Baldanno motioned with a crooked finger to bring it. Karl brought the soda and a glass from the corner cabinet and returned to his former position at the door. Needles opened the can, poured half into the glass. They watched in silence as Baldanno drank, his double chin below the heavy, dark beard cranked in the fluid. He made animal noises of satisfaction when he finished, wiped his lips with the back of his hand and spoke with a rasping voice.

"We invested big money with you." He raised his forefinger slowly and pointed at Vinnie, thrusting it at him. "You said everything was under control with this Zeist guy, and now you're telling me that there's fuckin' ten million slipping off ?"

Vinnie half stood. "It ain't slipped. . . ."

Charlie banged the table, sending the glass crashing to the cement floor. "Don't you fuckin' interrupt me until I'm finished." He motioned to the shattered glass. "You see what you made me do." He patted his stomach again. Needles leaped to the cabinet, brought another glass and filled it with the remaining soda.

Trentino looked down on the cement floor, his eyes on the tips of his shoes. This was a fucking trial, not a meet. He had brought them into a good deal, and now he was being treated like dog shit. He raised his head and met Karl's eyes. He could see the confusion on his face. Karl was probably wondering what the hell to do. Hold still while they steamroll me, or blast the fuckers? Poor dumb bastard. He turned his attention to the others. They watched. They knew. Hold still. Baldanna's graveled voice continued, paralyzing all possible action.

"Now where was I? The trouble with you, Vinnie, is you can't control your own backyard. You had a problem. Hey, we're family. Didn't we send help?"

Vinnie, his head bowed in respect, agreed. "You sent a good man."

Charlie banged the table again with his heavy fist. The Pepsi can rolled to the floor clattering to Karl's feet. "You're fucking-A we sent a good man! Tony The Barber was the best. We made our first bones together. I can't figger out what happened, takin' out a twerp kid. I can't figger it." He shoved his finger viciously at Trentino. "But you're responsible. You lissena me Vinnie. You clean up your act. You said it's gotta get finished by October 8th--take care of it! Don't send no errand boys like Angelo, or some dumb Polack who can't even tie his shoelaces. I woulda held still for a couple of hundred grand, maybe half a mill, but I ain't dropping no ten mill. If I do, it's your fuckin' ass."

Ten p.m. Frank came to help them pack and load up. He took the groceries in his car. The police had patrolled every street in every direction, north, south, east and west for twelve blocks. It looked clear. Maggie drove, Sara sat in the front seat next to her and Dev sat in the back, his head swiveling in every direction at each corner. The streets were deserted. The ride to 13th Avenue took only three minutes.

Vivien Stanton's house was at the foot of a dead end street facing the bay, overlooking Egg Harbor and the Longport Boulevard bridge. The house to the south shared the sandy approach to the docks which accommodated the three boats. One of the neighbor's and two of the Stantons'. Maggie pulled the Volvo along the side of the house, close to the main entrance door, to be unloaded then to remain hidden in the garage. The elegant grey wood siding shone in the moonlight, and the water reflected off the glass windows which rose from floor to ceiling, offering breath-taking views at sunrise and sunset. But for the present, their purpose was invisible sanctuary.

Maggie pressed the combination and opened the door. Invited, yes, but they felt like intruders as they mutely trudged up the spiral staircase to the second floor and sought out Sara's refuge. This was a good switch. No one would ever find them here. Only eight days to go. They would mark the calendar on the kitchen wall, a large X for each twenty-four hours. A week and a day.

Chapter 17

EIGHT days remaining. 6:30 A.M. They had given Sara the master bedroom with its floor to ceiling windows facing the bay, over which they had tightly drawn the drapes. The private bathroom with its shower that could handle five, the dressing area and the tub with a jacuzzi, all done in Sherle Wagner colors and designs were Vivien's pride and joy. Maggie had taken the room next to it, one she had occupied in the past. Devlin was relegated to the small den on the first floor.

Maggie slept less than an hour, tossing and turning, fully awakening from twilight dreams of terror. The face of Grey Eyes, Tony The Barber, had invaded her night. She dressed, quietly opened the door of the master bedroom, stood by the bed listening to the soft, rhythmical breathing of her daughter. Sara lay coiled, in the prenatal position, her fingers tightly gripping the blanket under her chin, White Bear nestled to her cheek, his flat, expressionless black eyes guarding her. Maggie slipped silently into the bathroom, brushed her teeth while staring at Sara's reflection in the mirror. Then she straightened the blanket, blew a kiss to her sleeping child and went down to the kitchen.

There was still some orange juice left from the 23rd Avenue food stock. She took half a glass, leaving the rest for Dev; Sara preferred the apple juice. Maggie, glass in hand, wandered around a room in which she had spent many happy moments. She stopped in front of the collage across from the kitchen counter. The early morning light cast changing shadows on the photos. In the center was Viv and Ken's wedding photo, Maggie as the maid of honor. The Stantons and the Crandalls standing side by side, Jessica's head tilted to Jonathan's and Ellen's controlled smile. Viv and Maggie, age twelve, in front of Pilgrim and again in Paris. Maggie and her husband, Howard, on the Stantons' boat. He wore jeans, a T-shirt and Ken's yachting cap. She wore a denim work shirt, tied at the waist, revealing her slender midriff. The picture had been taken five years ago. Only five years ago. She had been thirty-one.

Maggie had started her career in fabric design after college. Her first job sent her to the Merchandise Mart in Chicago. She found an opening at Brunschwig and Fils, advanced rapidly, her talent with colors and eye for innovative design drew the attention of the city's foremost interior designers. She was commissioned to create custom pieces for some of the wealthiest in the city. She was young, talented and attractive, with an impeccable family pedigree. She was invited to their homes and parties. So was Howard Mattson. He was handsome, authoritative and a successful stock broker. In certain ways, he reminded her of her father. They married within six months. She was twenty-four and he was forty-one. Howard Mattson had been married before, had two children, child support and alimony payments to make. Ellen had said he was too old for her. It wouldn't last. She was right.

Maggie lingered over the picture of her husband and herself. What did go wrong ? Maybe nothing was right in the first place. We were married for eleven years and were going our own ways after the second year. Oh, why did I waste so much of my life like that ? She held her head in her hands and closed her eyes. When she opened them, Devlin's reflection was in the window. Shc nodded, let her eyes slip from his and back to the collage.

Devlin put his finger on the pictures. "Who's the guy with you? The one in the sailor suit."

"That's Howard. My husband, Howard Mattson."

"Nice looking guy. How'd you happen to pick him?"

Her cheeks reddened with anger as she snapped at him. "Because you weren't around." She stared at the sea.

"I was around. When you came home, why didn't you call me?"

"The phone works both ways."

Devlin ran his finger over her picture. She was right. My damn pride wouldn't let me call. They kicked me out and then I'm supposed to crawl back for handouts? So she winds up with the guy in the sailor suit. Cut the crap, Devlin. It's not a sailor suit, it's a yachting cap. And the S.O.B. looks good in it. He tapped the glass frame.

"So what gives with Commander Mattson?"

"He's filing for divorce. Incompatibility."

"And?"

"I'm not contesting it."

She stepped to the window, pressed her face against the cool pane, her breath speckling the glass with small irregular clouds. Devlin went to her, and caressed her shoulders, bringing her back to his life. She turned, revealing her tear stained face.

"Mag, I thought, when you hugged me at Lennie Karp's house. . . ."

"It's was always so easy for you, so damn easy."

"That's what a lot of people think. But, no, it's not easy at all. When you left, I was all broken up. I love you, Mag. I always did, and I guess I always will." They folded into each other's arms with effortless, knowing movements and swayed gracefully as one. Her tears mingled with his, as their lips met, tingling with excitement and memories. His whisper danced in her ear.

"There's never been anyone but you."

She remained in his arms, pulled her head back, shook it emphatically and beamed a knowing smile. "That's *not* what I heard, Bobby Devlin." Then she brushed his wavy hair from his forehead and lovingly took his face between her hands. "But I will say this for you. You never got married."

The seventh day. Levy had completed his comments on the contract as discussed with Medford and it was ready for signature. He requested a signed set to forward to his client. Medford was happy to oblige. He attached the signature page signed by Zeist, properly witnessed and notarized, had it Fed Exed back to Levy with a cover letter stating that if a copy, fully executed by the seller, were not returned to him in forty-eight hours, the buyers interest was deemed to be at an end. Devlin had gotten the asking price of twenty million. Medford was confident the signed contract would be back on his desk the following day. He understood that it would take them at least a half a day to get the documents to the hidden girl.

An hour ago he had gotten a call from Trentino. What he didn't understand was Vinnie Trentino's insistence on seeing the papers. How did Trentino know the price of twenty million had been agreed upon? He heard Trentino's voice outside his door. Little Vinnie's arrival never required a formal announcement. Stanislaus Karlufsky's appearance or Trentino's raffish noises usually preceded him. Trentino's demeanor was different today. He was smiling. He either wanted something or must have successfully taken someone in a deal. Trentino extended his hand. Another landmark.

"Counselor, I got some good news for you. You got a contract for that piece of land all made up. I want you to give me a copy. But on my copy, I want you should make a small change. The price. Change it to two million."

Medford put his right hand behind him and wiped the palm on his back pocket. God knows what he might catch from that hood. "What is the purpose of changing thc agreed upon price, Vinnie?"

Trentino grinned broadly. Karlufsky saw his employer and followed with a foolish grin of his own. Vinnie brought forefinger to his nose, tapped it, and winked. "You should change the price because I'm gonna deliver it to you cheaper. I promise you that two million is what they're gonna sell it for."

Medford could not help but smile to himself. This indeed might be good news. What do we have to lose. He called in Ms. Walsh and asked her to take some dictation. Trentino, ever the gentleman, waved his hand for her to sit in the chair in front of Medford's desk.

"Ms. Walsh, please make the following changes in the Tyler land contract. There are only a few, and it shouldn't take you very long. Change the price from twenty million to two." She did not look up or question to confirm what she had heard. "Then add, on the last page, the following language. This agreement shall supersede any other agreement pertaining to the subject property. That's it. When you are done, copy three sets, put the red markers next to the signature lines and give them to Mr. Trentino."

Ms. Walsh said "thank you," nodded to Medford and Trentino and eased out of the room. Karl's head swiveled for maximum observation of her hips and legs as she exited. Medford returned to his desk, sat and pushed the black knight to threaten the white queen.

"Relax for a few minutes, Vinnie. She's very good and will bring the papers right in. It will take more time to copy than for her to produce it. Would you like a drink?"

Karl's face brightened. There was never a time of the day he would refuse whiskey. Vinnie shook his head and Karl frowned.

"What are you going to do with the contract when you get it? Do you know where the girl is?" Medford asked.

Vinnie smiled again and shook his head. "Not yet. But I ain't worried. I got a habit of bumping into people when I wanna find them."

Ms. Walsh returned with the documents, handed a

manila envelope with three sets to Trentino, one to Medford, nodded to Trentino and returned to her desk. Trentino waved farewell, sparing a relieved Medford of the handshake. He left the offices of Stern, Bradford and Altschuler and waited for the elevator. Trentino pressed the documents to his chest and laughed to himself. A two million dollar number. Only gonna cost us half. A million. That's what Charley Baldanno was ready to come up with. What the hell, he gets ten back. Ten for one. That's the number Baldanno is used to.

The sixth day. A routine had developed more easily here than on 23rd Avenue. For one thing, there were two bathrooms. Except for breakfast, all meals were taken together. Maggie wrote frequently in her journal, Sara sketched on Vivien's newsprint pad with the charcoal which lay about in abundance. Her drawings of the bay view outside the living room window and Maggie's profile displayed talent that impressed her parents. With each passing day, Maggie and Dev saw aspects of their daughter that helped them understand the joy she had brought to Trish and Alex.

Dev had patiently taught Sara casino and gin, but her favorite was Monopoly. The set sat on the living room floor, the game in progress, an uncompleted second day carry over. Maggie had traded her way into a monopoly of the Oranges, New York Avenue, St. James Place and Tennessee Avenue. She especially wanted Tennessee. That was where she had met Dev. She gave Sara fifteen hundred for it. He thought she overpaid.

Dev had many holdings, but no monopoly. Sara had Boardwalk and wanted Park Place. He gave it to her, no charge, as a gift for last year's birthday. He was making up for the time he wasn't around. That left Sara with enough cash to build houses and a hotel. And she did.

"Now, let's see. Houses are two hundred each, plus two hundred for a hotel." She calculated quickly. "That'll cost me six hundred for three houses on Park Place, and a thousand for the hotel on Boardwalk." She stripped herself of all her cash except for three yellow tens and one green twenty. "I'm calling my hotel The Palace. If you land on it, you owe me two thousand." She grinned happily at them. "Not quite twenty million, but it's a beginnnnnning!"

Devlin appraised his daughter. "You like the idea of having all that money, don't you? Doesn't that make us the same as The Max? Aren't we're just as greedy as he is?"

Sara was quick to respond. "No! We're different. We didn't kill anyone. And besides, he doesn't own it. This land belongs to the Tyler family. If he wants it, he pays for it."

Maggie patted Sara's head approvingly. Her daughter was talking like a true Tyler. Devlin observed the interchange. "Oh, yeah, you're right. It's Tyler land. I heard old Jeremiah really paid through the nose for it. Bought half of Absecon Island for five hundred bucks. Now The Max is offering millions for just a sliver, and you're still not satisfied. Right, ladies?"

Maggie let Sara answer. "He can afford it. He's rich. Everybody knows he's got zillions and girls chasing him on his yacht. Jamie showed it to me in People Magazine. He wants everything."

"You mean he wants to win," said Dev. "He wants to win all the marbles."

Sara nodded emphatically. "Right. So do I." She pondered the equity of it. "But if everybody wants to grab it all, how do you do it so it works out fair?"

Her parents didn't have the answer.

Trentino had tapped all his contacts, from every source he had ever used. What the hell good was having the contract, the money lined up, if he couldn't locate the kid. He was drawing blanks. Angelo had the best information network in the tri-state area and so far had come up with zilch. Little Vinnie ducked Baldanno's first call but he knew he was running out of time. Twenty-five years building up an organization, a good bundle socked away and now this crap. All over a piece of land the size of his backyard.

Chapter 18

THE fifth day. 10:00 a.m. Frank arrived at the 13th Avenue house with the contracts. Before leaving his office he had switched vehicles. He drove to Longport in a beat up Chevy pickup with a boat trailer hooked up in the rear and fishing poles sticking out the window. To complete his disguise, he wore extra large sun glasses and a black watch cap. He had two other detectives driving his car, which obviously had been identified. They were to circle the blocks around Berkley. The detective driving, who was built like Frank, wore Frank's jacket, his sunglasses and might have passed for Holenka. If Little Vinnie's boys had a tail on Frank, every minute of leeway counted. Time was not only money, it was life.

Dev ushered Frank into the dining room. The signing was going to be a ceremony of consequence. On the center of the table was a large drawing. Sara had sketched a hotel with "The Palace" emblazoned across its top. Next to it, where the sliver of land would have been located, she had placed an oreo. Under the cookie was a sign that bore the legend, "Sara's Twenty Million Dollar Birthday Cake." Sara sat serenely at the head of the table, the regal princess, the pen, her royal scepter, held high, poised for the official act. Maggie, the queen mother, stood behind Sara and was careful not to crack a smile.

"I feel very privileged to be invited to this birthday party," said Frank.

"My birthday party will be next week. This is my inheritance party," said Princess Sara.

Frank Holenka had a fifteen-year-old daughter. He was a quick study. He lay the papers on the table with a respectful air and stepped back. Devlin, the consort, opened the envelope, spread the pages and pointed to the signature lines for Maggie and Sara. They both signed with the proper decorum where indicated. Frank signed as a witness and Devlin notarized it. Tess could apply his notary seal in the office. They all took turns rubbing their fingers on Zeist's signature for luck. He had money, now they would. And it would be his. Half, anyway. Then there was shouting and screaming for joy. All except for Frank.

"I'm happy for you guys, that you got your signed contract and all, but why don't you hold the celebration until you got your hands on the bucks?"

Devlin tapped Holenka lightly with the documents. "Frank, stop being a cop for two minutes. We got five days to go and we're snug as a bug in a rug. Don't rain on the kid's parade."

Sara and Maggie were dancing around the room and stopped. Frank waved at them to continue. Sara took Maggie by the hand and pulled her up to the bedroom. "Come on, let me show you a house I saw in one of the magazines. We're going to buy it. Well, maybe we'll wait till I finish college." They loped up the stairs like two school girls.

Devlin watched till he could no longer see them, but didn't speak till their voices faded behind closed doors. "Frank, I'm a very lucky man."

"Stay that way and last this out. Everything under control? The alarm's set, you know who to call if some goon pops up at the last minute?"

"We're all set. And I had a good idea last night for another quick exit. Let's say, somehow, some way, we can't call the police or you, the bad boys are in front of the house and we're afraid to break the glass to set off the roof alarm because they might panic and start shooting, and we got our back to the bay."

"This better be good."

"It's really quite simple, Detective Holenka. Maggie and I are both pretty handy with boats. If Trentino's got his goons out front, we jump out the back porch, across a fifty yard stretch of beach and hop into one of the Stanton boats that are docked out there. Then we either shoot across the bay to Egg Harbor or hug the shoreline, call you on the portable phone and meet you where you tell us where to get off." Devlin leaned against the dining room table, took a mock drag from an imaginary cigarette and flicked away the invisible ashes.

"Not a bad emergency fall-back plan. Where's the portable phone now?"

Devlin pointed to it lying on the sofa, near the TV.

"Very good Mr. Devlin. Wouldn't it be better if it were in the boat?"

Devlin smacked his forehead. "Geez, Frank, that's why you're the captain of detectives. I'll do it right now while you're here. Is it okay to go out?"

"Yeh, nobody was on the street. Check out the boat. I'll wait till you get back before I leave."

Devlin took the boat ignition key from the kitchen key drawer, the portable phone and some bottled water. He eased open the front door and took in a deep breath of fresh air. It was wonderful. There were two boats. The Lady Di, an elegant older craft belonging to Ken's sister, was docked there and not very fast. Vivien's boat was a year old and had all the latest features. He hopped onto the newer boat, inserted the key in the ignition and the good craft *Viva Viv* started like a dream. He put the phone in the bait station, the bottled water in the rope locker in the bow and walked to the stern to see if all was in order. One of the harpoons had fallen off its bracket under the gunnels on the port, and a gaff was lying on the deck on the starboard. He set them back in place and checked the life preservers. Okay. You look ship-shape, *Viva Viv,* hope we don't have to use you this week. He returned to the house. Frank left with the documents to be delivered to Tess and the wheels of progress were cranking.

The fourth day. Trentino could no longer avoid Baldanno's twice daily calls. Little Vinnie was asked if he needed help again, but in any event, Baldanno was sending someone. Vinnie called Baldanno and wanted to be left alone.

"Charlie, I tole you, I'm gonna handle it."

Baldanno screamed into the phone. "You got four fuckin' days left. You blow the ten mill, you blowin' two and half mill a day."

He had it up to his neck. Vinnie screamed back. "Stop gettin so fuckin' hot. If I gotta do it, I'll do it personal. Just keep fuckin' cool." Trentino regretted the words as soon as they left his mouth.

Baldanno did not scream. His tone carried a more ominous message. "You tellin' me to keep cool, Vinnie. Awright. Maybe we all stay cool." He hung up.

Trentino knew the story. A Detroit restaurant owner had borrowed from Baldanno and not paid after two extensions of the loan. When pressed by Baldanno, the restaurateur told Needles he was good for the loan and Charley should keep cool. The next day employees of the restaurant found him in the meat freezer, hung next to a side of beef. There was a note on his face "to keep cool." The ice pick in his forehead kept the note from falling off.

Ms. Walsh accepted the hand delivered package, noted the return address and knew Mr. Medford would be pleased to have it. She tapped softly on his door, entered and placed it on his desk. Medford was about to complain of thc interruption to his phone conversation until he recognized Albert

Levy's return address. He had instructed Ms. Walsh to bring these to him immediately upon arrival. He terminated his conversation abruptly, it was only with Rickie Murdock. He ripped open the envelope with one hand and pressed Zeist's automatic direct dial number with the other. He raced to the signature page. He had done it! He felt elated, lifted to humor. A rare status.

"Max, I have it."

In a half laugh, he had shouted. Zeist didn't know who it was.

"Addison?"

"Yes, yes, Addison. Your faithful and effective attorney, Addison Grant Medford, the Third, Esquire." He felt drunk. It was exhilarating. "I have in my hot little fingers the answer to your dreams and our problems. A fully signed, sealed contract for that damn little piece of land. The title company called earlier and approved, but I didn't call you till we had this."

Zeist was almost as pleased as Medford, but this was not his first victory. Nothing is ever as sweet as that. He twirled the gold coin, stopping it before he could see it come up heads or tails. He knew he would get what he wanted.

"Fine job, Addison. Well done. We've got it locked up for twenty million."

"I can't give you an explanation because I don't have one, but another client of mine came to the office three days ago, and asked for a copy of this contract. I gave it to him with the requested price reduction to two million."

"Very interesting. We'll just have to wait and see if we're paying two or twenty."

The third day. Despite the tension in counting the remaining hours of the next three days, an unexpected feeling of peace surrounded them. In less then a month, the crucible they lived in had forged them into a family. Devlin began to understand why his mother and brother, Danny, prayed. Only two more days to go and he would have everything in the world he wanted. It was so close, he was sure they would make it.

4:30 in the afternoon. The lowering sun splashed its brilliance upon the bay. Sara tried to capture some of the colors in a seascape. Maggie napped on the couch and Dev watched his daughter. He had very few treasures, but he had brought one of them with him, tucked away in his duffel bag.

"Sara."

"Uh huh." She didn't look up. She had wet the paper so the colors would run and painted speedily, protecting the white spaces she had left where the water would crest into waves. Dev watched in fascination as her hand danced over the work, sweeping all into the desired image. She stopped for a minute to appraise her progress and shook her head disapprovingly.

Well, he liked it. "Sara, I have a pre-birthday present for you. It's not much compared to your inheritance." He opened her hand and placed a small ball of tissue paper wrapped around a hard, round object. "I hope you like it. It's something that means a lot to me."

She carefully unfolded the tissue. Inside was an oval locket of gold, no bigger than a fifty cent piece, hung on a gold chain as thin as a hair. A tiny bit of an emerald in its center. Sara opened the antique and admired the photo of a young girl with eyes like Dev's. "It's beautiful. I love it. Is that your mother?" Dev nodded. "Where is the locket from?"

"From her home in Ireland. A place called Castlebar, in County Mayo."

Sara held it up to her neck. "What was your mother's name?"

"Maureen."

Sara smiled over the coincidence. "That's my middle name."

"I know."

5:00 p.m. Jonathan arrived at his home and entered his bedroom to change from golf clothes as the phone rang. He ran to get it. Penny Linden was back in town. They had a date tonight that he dreamt about nightly. He answered with his sexiest voice. The response was a major disappointment. It wasn't Penny.

"Hellooooh, Jonathan, how wonderful you sound. Have you been exercising?" He was so frustrated he was speechless. "Jonathan, it's Jessica. Are you there?"

"Yes, I'm here, I just got in and I'm dashing out again." Why does this woman call every time I'm in a rush?

"Is everything all right, Jonathan? Can I help you with anything?"

"No, Jessica, everything is fine. I hope you're fine too, and Viv and Ken are well, I assume?" We'll get the family status covered then maybe I can get the hell out of here.

"Why bother asking me about Vivien? She calls me once in a blue moon. Especially now that she's in London. If you want to know about Vivien, ask Margaret. Your daughter probably gets more phone calls from Vivien than I do. She *is* staying at Vivien's house in Longport."

Jonathan sat on the bed. So that's where they disappeared to. He reached for a pencil and paper as Jessica rambled on.

"Honestly, Jonathan, for the life of me I cannot understand why she is staying at Vivien's." Jessica tittered. "What's the matter, Jonathan, can't Margaret bring visitors to your house? So you see, everyone seems to be having a good time but me. *You* never call anymore. You should, you know. Didn't we have a lovely evening at the club buffet?"

"Yes, yes, yes. We certainly did have a lovely time. Oh, Jess, darling, I wanted to stop and see Margaret. She wants me to bring her some things from the house. I misplaced Viv's address. Have you got it handy?" He tapped the bed anxiously waiting for the response.

"Oh, I can never remember the phone number. It's so impossible, what with having them all punched in that automatic dialing."

OH, GOD, THIS WOMAN IS MADDENING! He said it slowly and sweetly. "Just the address, Jessica, dear."

"The address. It's Seventeen 13th Avenue in Longport. I always remember that because I was seventeen when I met Alfred and exactly four years before. . . ."

"Thank you so much, Jessica, but I've got to run now. I'll call you tomorrow." He hung up, took Medford's card from his wallet and dialed the direct line number.

Ms. Walsh answered. "Mr. Medford's office."

"Ms. Walsh, this is Jonathan Crandall. I have some information that Mr. Medford is anxious to have. May I speak with him please."

"He's in a partners meeting now and that usually isn't finished until six. They don't like interruptions unless, of course, you think it's urgent."

Crandall looked at his watch. 5:15. It could wait until tomorrow morning. One more day for a closing wouldn't matter, and Medford will have to speak with Margaret to push the matter through.

"Well, I suppose at this hour, it could wait a day. Tell him I have my daughter's current address. She's staying at a friend's house. The name is Stanton. Her phone number is in the book. No, that's her maiden name. I forgot her married name. I'll get it for Mr. Medford tomorrow when he calls me."

"Do you have the address, Mr. Crandall? Mr. Medford might want to FedEx her some documents."

"You're right. Anything to keep the wheels rolling. It's Seventeen 13th Avenue, Longport. By the way, Ms. Walsh, what are you doing in the office at this time ? Aren't you girls usually out like a shot when the clock strikes five?"

"I'm just a working girl trying to do my job."

"Do you think you might break away to join me for

lunch one day?"

"I'd enjoy that very much, Mr. Crandall."

"Jonathan. Call me Jonathan. Please tell Mr. Medford to call me tomorrow and you have a good evening." He hung up, rubbed his hands in anticipation of the many good things to come. Not the least of which was the evening he would be spending with Penny Linden.

Betty Walsh had the 13th Avenue address carefully written out to be placed with the covering memo on Medford's desk. He already had a signed contract, could proceed with his business and she didn't think he would be that interested in Margaret Crandall's address now. But her other employer would. There was only one day left. She dialed Angelo's number.

Trentino was tracked down and the call was connected to his car within three minutes. Karl answered.

"Boss, Angelo wantcha."

Trentino yanked the phone from Karlufsky's hand. "This better be something good, you're taking me down to the friggin' wire."

"We got 'em located. I checked the address on the map. It's a dead end street a few blocks from the Point in Longport. I sent Carmine and Big Mike to box it up, make sure nobody gets in or out."

Vinnie whistled and grudgingly shook his head in admiration. Right under our nose. The kid misses a hit with the car bomb, then almost gets knocked off by Tony. Instead of skipping for parts unknown, they go under ten blocks away. That takes a lotta balls. Smart. But they ain't playin' with friggin' kids. It's gonna be payoff time. Trentino decided his plan. He didn't shout at Angelo. He spoke in the cool calculating measured beat of the commander of his forces.

"Here is what I want you to do. Have Petie, our phone guy, make a repair on the street. Check the alarm setup, find out what's with the cops, any watch, regular patrols. If you need help with the local cops, get the guys in Trenton to push the right buttons. If they're gonna make a run for it, I wanna know how they could do it, which way they could go. Don't fuck up. I'll be there in fifteen minutes and I'm gonna want a lot of answers."

Karl got Trentino back to the office in twelve minutes, but Vinnie didn't get all the answers he wanted. Angelo was impressed with Vinnie's patience. He only threw one ashtray and busted a lamp. Two hours later he had all the hard information he wanted.

The location of the prey was confirmed. Carmine, using a surveillance cam, had spotted all three of them in the house. No cops were stationed on guard. Two scheduled patrols went by, one at nine in the morning and one at seven at night, and two unscheduled patrols. Trentino ruled their cars should be limited to one, otherwise too much attention. The phone line and alarm system were hooked into the police station. Petie had given Karl a simple drawing with instructions. Tear off the phone lines marked in red on the side of the house and the phone was dead and one of the alarm systems was deactivated. That was the good news. The second alarm system was on the roof of the house, and would take over an hour to deactivate. Any breaking of the windows would set off the alarm, then you got a Mexican standoff because sure as shit you don't want any witnesses to the hit. Recommendation: get the kid out of the house, make sure Vinnie is away from the scene and drop her in a car accident. If they try to run, their best bet is to try to escape by water. There were two boats docked on the bay. Deactivate the boats or have a faster boat.

Vinnie made a few calls and a decision for his troops.

"Angelo, get me the fastest boat you can get your hands on. I know how to handle them. The Scarab is a good one. A pal of mine uses one for bringing shit into Florida. Karl, you gonna take over for Carmine and Big Mike. I'm gonna take a cruise. You drive there in the Mercedes. Get there tomorrow morning at six thirty, rip off the wires that knock out the phone, and then wait for me.

Karl was confused. "You mean, not now?"

"No, you dumb, dickhead. I just tole ya. Tomorrow morning at six. They ain't going nowhere. The kid ain't gonna be eighteen for twenty-four hours. We got plenty of time."

Chapter 19

DEV was up and dressed at seven. He heard his women upstairs. He was sure nobody in this house had slept very well last night. The tension of survival had taken its toll. Now it was down to hours, not days or weeks. At the stroke of midnight, Sara would be eighteen. He breathed a deep sigh. They were going to make it. He knew it. It was a very, very special day. Maybe he should shave? The roar of a boat's engine shattered the hushed morning air. It was very close to the house. Dev's heart leaped as he raced to the kitchen.

Devlin saw him through the glare of the early sun, getting out of the boat, onto the dock, his shoes sinking slightly in the damp sand. Little Vinnie Trentino shaded his eyes, peered at Devlin framed in the large window, smiled and waved a greeting with the briefcase in his hand. Devlin wrenched the phone out of its cradle. *Dead!* The sweat ran down his back. Oh, Jesus, only sixteen hours to go. He returned the worthless phone and spotted Karl running to Trentino, proudly flicking torn phone wires.

They advanced onto the back porch, eye to eye with Devlin, only separated by the large glass window. Trentino held up the briefcase, offering as one would a house gift, and shouted through the thick glass. Devlin hated that face, one he would have known even if Frank had not shown him the picture.

"Been lookin' all over for you. Got a great surprise for the kid."

Devlin shouted in return. "She's had enough surprises for a lifetime. One of them was a car bomb that killed the two most important people in her life."

Maggie and Sara, drawn by the shouting, had descended the stairs. Sara, half hidden behind Maggie, whimpered. "Oh, no, no, no! Make them go away, please."

Devlin waved a comforting hand behind his back to Sara and stood his ground, never breaking eye contact with Trentino. "Don't worry, Sara, they're not going to come inside."

He shouted louder, affirming that Trentino was getting his message. "Little Vinnie knows that if he breaks the glass, the roof alarm will go off and the police would be here before he might do anything foolish. Isn't that right, Vinnie?"

Trentino smiled and nodded in confirming Devlin's conclusion. This must be the guy with the balls. And he's smart. Let's see if he's smart enough to get out of this alive. "Lissen, buddy, don't hook me up with that car bomb lunatic. We would never do anything like that. I don't even know the guy."

Trentino opened the briefcase, gave Devlin a quick view of its contents and shut it. "I'm a responsible businessman. We just came here to give you money for the land you wanna sell. Let me tell you my proposition. Hey, open the window, I'm gettin a sore throat from shoutin'." He smiled again. "Come on, this is no way to do business."

Devlin played the game, also smiled, held up his hand and mouthed, "Wait a minute." Sara backed off to the stairs as he conferred with Maggie. They had tested the small louvered window next to the picture window. When open, the louvered window let in the ocean breeze. It would allow conversation and could be closed in seconds to reconnect the alarm system. Devlin returned to Trentino and shouted his message.

"I'm going to open this little window and we'll listen to your proposition. It can be closed in a second and then we're just back to square one."

Vinnie smiled his broadest smile of the day. He made rolling circles with his hands to open the window. Devlin opened the louvers an inch, allowing the ocean breeze to carry in the voice of his enemy.

"You were asking two mill, which is a damn good score, for the piece of dirt and then you figure you got us by the balls, so you ask for twenty. But to show you we're good people, we're not gonna hold it against you that you got greedy, and we're gonna give you the two mill you asked for in the first place." Vinnie patted the briefcase.

"Yeh," said Devlin. "But two, ain't twenty."

"You don't have the twenty mill. They just promise you that on a contract. I'm sincere, baby. I brought some of mine to hand over today."

Sara edged forward, peering at the briefcase. "Is that real money in there?"

Vinnie quickly opened the case and thrust it forward. Stacked layers of currency, a sea of green Benjamin Franklins stared at Sara. Talk of money is exciting, the sight of it, hypnotic. Vinnie watched Sara's eyes roll over row after row of hundred dollar bills.

"This is as real as they make it, sweetheart. Five hundred thou." He pointed to Sara's Mainland High T-shirt. " You could buy enough of those for every kid in the country and you wouldn't put a dent in your bankroll."

Maggie pulled Sara back to her, but Vinnie knew they were listening. He continued the pitch.

"You keep this half a mill, I bring you the other one and a half when we close. If you wanna keep it all in cash, under the table and not pay taxes – hey, I could accommodate you. You don't get hurt with taxes, I got some loose cash. So, maybe Uncle Sam gets hurt a little bit. But what the hell, he can afford it, and they screw up with the taxpayer's money anyway."

He examined each of their faces as he finished. They were trying it on. The sight of green always works. It gets 'em every time. Better than sex.

"So, whattya say? We do it nice and friendly, right?" He took the contract out of the flap in the briefcase above the cash, and held it up. "The two ladies come out and sign this contract, I give you this box full of moola now, and we're in business."

Devlin eyed the contract and recognized the initials on the bottom. "Hold the contact closer to the window. I just want to glance at something." Vinnie did and Devlin read what he wanted to. "Okay, Vinnie, shove it through the louvered window."

Karl growled. "Shove it up your ass."

Vinnie's voice was low, not threatening. "Let the ladies sign it. We need the kid to come with us, to our lawyer for an hour, to have her signature notarized. And some other legal stuff because she is a minor. Don't worry, hey, we're not gonna hurt the kid. I'm a business man. I swear on my mother's grave."

"Oh, did you have a mother?"

Karl's hand ran to his jacket. Vinnie clamped onto Karl's wrist, halting any explosion and continued to mediate. "Hey, sport. What's your name? Devlin, yeah, Bobby Devlin, that's right. Bobby, you got this all wrong. Whattya think this is – a snatch?"

He dropped the briefcase to the porch floor, threw his head back and laughed uproariously. Karl observed and joined in. Trentino continued. "Some helluva snatch. You wind up with my money and I wind up with your kid. That's a helluva reverse snatch. Whattya wanna do now, count the money?"

Devlin countered. "I'm a notary, I can take their signatures."

Vinnie's laughter was quickly united by Karl's. Vinnie stopped his abruptly, followed by Karl. Trentino's eyes turned black, his voice was flat, void of human quality.

"You're a notary, huh. You also the president of the United States? I want the mother to sign this. Send the kid out."

They all stood silent, acknowledging the stalemate, waiting for the opponent's next move. Devlin, his eyes glued to Vinnie and Karl, heard Sara's hurried breathing behind him. The negotiation was over.

"You made your point, Vinnie. Can we go upstairs and talk it over? Give us five minutes?"

Vinnie shrugged. "Take ten."

They climbed the spiral staircase in measured beat, Maggie and Sara hand in hand, Devlin two steps away, entered the master bedroom and closed the door. Maggie and Sara sat on the edge of the bed, still comforted by each other's hands, and waited for Devlin to speak.

"I saw the front page of the contract. It still is Medford's form, the Stern, Bradford computer entry is at the bottom of the page, but Little Vinnie Trentino changed more than the price. He also changed the name of the Buyer from Emzee Hotel Holdings, that's The Max, to Brandywine Capital. That's probably him. He's going to buy it from us for two million, screw Zeist and sell it for twenty."

Sara slapped the bed cover. "What a crook! How do we know they won't kill us and keep it all?"

"I just explained that to you. I don't think he'd do that if he could buy it for two and sell it for twenty."

Sara mulled it over. "And if I make it till tomorrow. I get the twenty million?"

Dev nodded.

Maggie took Sara's hand back into hers. "I don't care. I think we should sign it. We're trapped here."

"Maybe not," said Dev.

Both women spoke, "What do you mean?"

"In the first place, we really don't know what they are going to do. In the second place, I don't trust Trentino as far as I can throw his big gorilla."

Maggie threw up her hands in desperation. "Dev, what's the difference, we can't get out of here."

"Listen, please listen. I've got an idea that might work. If, somehow, someway, I can convince Trentino and Karl to go along, get rid of their guns, we might try an end run. They want Sara. That's why they're here. Maggie, you and Sara look enough alike to be sisters. They've had a look at both of you and a close-up of Sara. Maggie, if you put on Sara's Mainland High T-shirt, her shorts, sunglasses and a kerchief over your head, just enough blonde hair sticking out, you would fool me. Especially if you were running."

"Where will she run to? They'll shoot her," said Sara.

"Let me finish. Sara, you hide yourself somewhere upstairs. Maggie, when, if, I call you, come running downstairs, disguised as Sara, and head for the boat. The Viva Viv. Here's the key. I put the cellular phone in the bait locker. It's right on top. Grab it, start the boat and head across the bay to Egg Harbor. As soon as you're moving, call Frank, and the local cops. Here's Frank's numbers and the local police. I'm going to try to get Vinnie to wait in the car, but if he starts to chase you in his boat, which is a Scarab and fast as hell, turn back to our shoreline. If you have to get off, he'll know the police are coming and won't do anything. Anyway he won't have a gun, otherwise I wouldn't have called you down in the first place."

Maggie stood and put her hands on hips confronting Devlin. "You just didn't think of this, did you? You've been mulling this over for days."

Dev nodded slowly. "Well, are you game? I think we should do it. Shall we vote?"

Sara also stood. "My vote is with Dad."

Dev stirred with pride over Sara's affirmation of his fatherhood. Maggie made it unanimous. He went downstairs for his confrontation and Maggie started her disguise.

Trentino pointed at his watch as Devlin approached

the window. "You asked for five minutes, I give you ten and you come down in twelve. I'm running out of patience. You don't get it do you, you dumb Mick? You think it's just the money? Yeh, you're friggin' A, it's a big part of it. But understand this – even my stupid Polack Karl understands it. When I was eight years old, this kid, Johnnie Jacowsky, another dumb Polack like Karl here, knocks my head off and takes my money. It takes me a few years, but I get him. Since then, nobody, *nobody* beats Vinnie Trentino. You think your tinny alarm or the cops are gonna stop me?"

"I told you before, Vinnie, you had a point. We can work out a deal."

Vinnie bit the inside of his lip to keep from smiling. Show 'em the green and then a little muscle and they come around. "What's on your mind?"

"I'm sure you are sincere and a man of your word, Vinnie, but I confess I'm a bit worried about Karl's sincerity. I have a vague suspicion that the bulge in your jacket is a gun. I have no idea what's creating the bulge in his pants."

Karl had a feeling he was being insulted, but wasn't sure. "Vinnie, what the fuck is he talking about? I'm gonna waste this guy."

"Shut up, Karl. So, whattya want him to do ?"

"I want him to take the gun out of *your* jacket, remove the bulge from *his* jacket, walk to the end of the pier, and drop his gun and your gun into the bay. Then, I want him to get into the boat on the left, get some rope from the rope locker, and bring it back here."

Karl looked at Vinnie for instructions. "Go ahead, Karl. Do what he said."

Karl took the gun from Vinnie's jacket, went to the end of the dock and dropped it along with his own gun into the water. Trentino wiped his hands back and forth, denoting the act had been accomplished. "You satisfied? We don't want to hurt nobody. You gonna call the two broads down now?"

"Not quite yet. I'm waiting for Karl to come back

with the rope. Then you tie him up and I call down the girls."

"You want me to tie him up? Whattya afraid of him? He's harmless. He's just a big baby."

"I hope he can find the rope. It's in the locker, marked 'rope locker.' Can he read?"

"Yeh, yeh, he can read. Not good like me, but he can read."

Karl returned with the rope. Devlin glanced at his watch. He had gained more than enough time for Maggie to change. "Okay, Vinnie, you tie him up, wait in the car, I call the girls and the show is on the road."

Trentino hefted the rope in his hand. In his gut he didn't like this. "I dropped the guns, expensive ones, in the bay like you wanted. And I'm gonna tie up Karl. But if you're getting fucking cute, you gonna regret it for the rest of your life, which may not be very long."

Devlin felt the sweat roll down his back, under his arms. He watched Trentino tie Karl's hands behind his back. There was another yard of rope hanging off the end. "Tell Karl to lie down, tie the end of the rope around his legs. I don't want him to kick me when you leave with Sara and I'm left baby-sitting him."

Karl submitted, cursing Devlin under his breath. Vinnie whistled happily as he tightened the knots on Karl's wrists, patted the prone body, dusted off his hands and put the closed briefcase next to the window.

Devlin pointed to the briefcase. "I'm sure you didn't take it out while we were upstairs, but do you mind if I see the money again."

Vinnie gave Devlin a look of disbelief that anyone could doubt his honorable conduct. He flicked open the cover, confirmed the contents and closed the lid. "Good. Now if you'll wait in the car, in five minutes Sara will be down to meet you."

Trentino looked at his watch. "Five minutes. Don't make it six. Hey, Karl, don't do the polka while you waiting. Don't worry, somebody will be here for you right away." He whistled again as he walked to the car.

Devlin opened the porch door, watched and waited for Trentino to get into the car, quickly stuffed his handkerchief in Karl's mouth, ran to the stairs and shouted for Maggie. Maggie in Sara's T-shirt, raced through the kitchen. They kissed in passing. His heart beat wildly, far more than in any race he had run in his life. *Run, Mag, run, run, run!* Good luck, my darling, Maggie. He sped to the rail of the deck, saw her board the *Viva Viv* and get the phone. Devlin didn't see Karl spit out the handkerchief. But he spun around at the sound of Karl's shrieks.

"Vinnie, Vinnie, the kid got out! She's on the boat!"

Trentino's car tore up the sand driveway and screeched to a halt. He leaped out, fired a shot at Maggie's figure, now at the helm, and turned to fire one at Devlin. Dev felt a stab across his left arm. Son of a bitch, son of a bitch! He had another gun hidden in the damn car! Maggie started the Viva Viv and pulled away. Trentino leaped out of his car and ran toward the Scarab. I've got to stop him before he gets into the Scarab, Devlin realized. He'll catch Mag. Oh, please, God, please, don't let her get hurt. Devlin vaulted the side of the porch. His right foot sank in the wet sand, imbedded deeply from the leap. His left arm burned as he desperately wrapped both hands around the entangled leg to pull it free. The sand, heavy with water, was like cement. The suction at the bottom refused to release him. Trentino had reached the Scarab. Oh, God, please let me escape. Devlin tore at the sand, pulling away handfuls over bleeding knuckles. The Scarab's motor sputtered. Hope crept into Devlin's heart. Mother in heaven, don't let it start. He pulled with all the strength in his body, fell backwards and yanked his foot clear of the mud. The Scarab's motor roared, shot out to the bay, and the hunt commenced.

Devlin raced to the dock and boarded the Lady Di. Maybe he could leap onto the Scarab as it passed. Maybe there is a gun, a gaff, a harpoon, anything to use for a weapon. I know I don't deserve it, but Maggie does. Let me be lucky, just this once. There it was. Under the gunnel, a rusty harpoon. Devlin grasped it and ran to the bow. The Scarab increased its pursuit of Maggie. Devlin reached the bow, poised, harpoon in hand for the throw of his life. Keep your balance, stay steady, this is not the Shamrock, this is not just a game of darts. Dev, this is for all that counts, for all that matters in your life. *You can do it!*

The Scarab approached the Lady Di, waves broke the water, shifting Devlin's stance from side to side. Damn you, Vinnie. Devlin grabbed at the railing, planted his legs firmly and prepared for the throw. Don't miss! There's just one shot. Trentino was only sixty feet away and advancing rapidly. He spotted the figure above him, spit in contempt and raised his gun. Devlin hurled the harpoon with all the strength in his body, all the hate in his soul, his arm extended fully, to send the shaft true to its mark, and let the momentum of the throw flatten his body to the rail. Trentino's gun shot sailed past him. The harpoon found its target. Devlin heard the groan and the sound of snapping bone. Devlin raised his head to see the blood rush from Trentino's chest, the white shirt rapidly turn to crimson, the red spittle run from his mouth. Trentino vainly struggled to pull the harpoon from his body, the barbed hook had set. His face contorted in agony as he lurched forward and fell over the railing into the sea. The unattended Scarab steering wheel spun wildly, sending the craft in a series of circles, shifting toward the docks along the shore. It reached the first one at breakneck speed and crashed. The explosion shattered the windows of the house in front of the dock. Flames skyrocketed to the sky as the waves lapped at the burning wreckage.

Maggie saw the conflagration, took the kerchief from her head, waved it to Dev and set the *Viva Viv* homeward bound. Unseen by Maggie or Dev, Sara had watched from the second story of rear window, and had seen the drama unfold. She, too, waved her family home.

Chapter 20

THE police and Frank were on their way within one minute of Maggie's calls. The locals arrived three minutes after the shooting was over. Frank, who was in AC, sped through every traffic light on the main drag in Ventnor and Margate. He got there in twenty. The emergency medics examined Dev's arm injury. Luckily, Vinnie was not a very good shot. It was only a minor flesh wound above the elbow and would heal easily.

Sara embraced them both when they came back to the house. They had saved her life again. The danger was finally, truly, over and done with. Frank, however, insisted on heavy police guard around the clock until they left tomorrow morning. Dev was too weary to battle the demand.

"Okay, Frank, if it makes you happy. What ever you say. I'm bushed."

When Frank and the locals cleared out, the three acknowledged their faded adrenaline. The socket had been pulled on the electric cord of energy. At nine-thirty in the morning, they all slipped off to nap. Maggie on her bed, Sara on the sofa in front a droning TV, and Dev in the same kitchen chair, where he sat earlier enduring the medic's ministrations.

At ten-thirty, Sara awakened to the sound of trucks and voices. The TV, left on all night, flashed a picture of the house. Vickie Reardon, a news reporter for WMGM TV40, had mentioned Sara's name. Sara shook her head and rubbed her eyes, attempting to comprehend what was happening.

"Dev, wake up! Wake up! We're on TV. Maggie, come down."

Maggie ran down the stairs, fearing another crisis had arisen. It hadn't. Unless media exposure was it. Ms. Reardon was broadcasting from the front of the house. They could almost hear her voice from the outside as well as the TV.

"Approximately three hours ago, this peaceful view in Longport overlooking the Great Egg Harbor Bay was the scene of violence and death."

The three stood transfixed, feeling removed from the very details and events they had experienced. It couldn't be them, it was on TV. The familiar name of Vincenzo, Little Vinnie Trentino, the recent car bomb in Linwood to which this event might be related, and the discovery of a briefcase containing a large but unspecified sum of money, were all too bizarre to be a part of their lives. The reporter continued:

"A facet that makes this story even more news worthy is the unsolicited statement just released from the offices of Maxwell "The Max" Zeist. According to the Zeist spokesman, Emzee Hotel Holdings, one of the many Zeist entities, has contracted to purchase a small parcel of land from Ms. Crandall and Ms. Johnson."

A picture of Sara in her Mainland High cheerleader outfit flashed on the screen. Sara gasped.

"The reported price is twenty million. The Max stated that he was pleased to hear that no harm had come to anyone here today and the ladies will enjoy their millions. More details on the evening news. This is Vickie Reardon, reporting to you from Longport, New Jersey."

The regular programming resumed, Sara snapped off the TV and danced around the living room.

"Wait till I tell Jamie I was on TV. That picture they

put on, my hair looked terrible. I've gotta call her. Hey, the phone is working. They must have fixed it."

Maggie and Dev smiled with pleasure at these first signs of return to teenage normalcy. Sara called Jamie, who was still in school. She spoke to Phyllis Matthews. Of course Jamie would call her back, but when was Sara to return to their house? Or to her house? Sara shrugged and said she would call and let the Matthews know.

After the news break, Frank told Tess the coast was clear. The Longport phone number spread like wildfire and the phone rang incessantly for the rest of the morning. Jonathan Crandall had the number since yesterday, but he didn't call till later that afternoon. Not until Penny Linden left for the airport. The surprise call of the day was from Maxwell Zeist. Sara answered the phone and quickly handed it over to Devlin.

Zeist, the consummate hustler, oozed good will. "Bob Devlin, I've heard wonderful things about you from Addison Medford. Tell that lucky young lady, Sara, we're most happy for her good fortune and we're going to put real icing on her cake. I understand she has an important birthday coming up."

"Yes, Mr. Zeist. Tomorrow is her eighteenth."

"Not Mr. Zeist, call me, Max."

"Well then, why don't you just call me, Bob?"

"Bob, tell Sara we are preparing a birthday party for her tomorrow in the Grand Ballroom of The Palace Hotel. She can invite as many guests as she pleases, dinner will be at seven. If there is a particular musical group Sara wants, call Beth Wilson, my entertainment manager and she'll try to get them. We're having the closing on the sale in two days, so why don't you, Bob, and Ms. Crandall and of course, the birthday girl, stay at the hotel. We can arrange the presidential suite, or if you prefer, a suite for the girls and one for you. My limo will drive you back and forth to Philadelphia for the closing. You can sleep at the hotel before and after the party. Just relax and have fun!"

Dev had to admit it. He was smooth and he was the maximum.

"What can I say, Max. You convinced me. Yes. I think the party idea is great, and the presidential suite sounds cozy, but let me check with the ladies. Get back to you, Max."

It was sounding like party time. Dev related the conversation. The family took a vote, decided to accept The Max's offer and prepared for the next two days. They would sleep in Longport, get up early, and hasten to the luxury at The Palace Hotel by noon. The rest of that day was spent inviting guests for the party, and the girls deciding what to wear.

The family vote was for the presidential suite. It had become more than comfortable living together and the suite had two bathrooms. First there was the stop at the respective residences and the inevitable delay caused by rethinking feminine clothing decisions. Dev's was simple. Tie or no tie. The ride over to The Palace was filled with happy expectation.

The presidential suite was mind-boggling. Fresh flowers in every room, a lavish basket of fruit and chilled champagne greeted them in the living room. It would be two hours until the party guests arrived. They discussed the future. The pattern of a family discussion and a vote had become a happy and binding habit. Maggie would move in with Sara at 59 Berkley. There, she would still be close enough to finish her last year at Mainland High. She had made early application to Skidmore and the University of Pennsylvania and had been accepted by both.

"I hope you pick U. of P.," said Maggie. "It's closer, you can come home more often and we can visit more frequently."

Dev was glad to hear Mag say "we." He was to stay at his apartment. It was close enough, and Maggie preferred it. At least until her divorce was over.

The sign in front of the Grand Ballroom read "SARA

M. JOHNSON PARTY." The decor was tasteful and elegant. No mammoth happy birthday banner was in sight. Dazzling arrays of flowers were in abundance, along with a Baccarat bowl filled with Beluga caviar and shrimp the size of horseshoes. The entree choices were imported Dover sole, filet mignon or squab. Desserts were endless and the service outstanding.

The guests included Jamie, Phyllis and Ed Matthews, Evie and David Conroy, Frank and Helene Holenka, Jake and Arlene Balaban, Pop Devlin, who was thrilled to meet this new granddaughter, and Jonathan Crandall, who put in an appearance with Jessica Stanton. Tess and Marty Donahue couldn't make it. Tess had the baby at four in the afternoon. The baby was named Claire, after her grandmother. Tess promised to bring the baby to the office in a month and Dev could be surrounded by another female.

Two tables were filled with Sara's school friends. Dev liked them all except Todd Ansen. He was the Mainland High football hero, an all-state quarterback, who kept hugging Sara and telling her how great she looked. Yes, she did, but Devlin considered that beside the point. Sara hugged him back and told Maggie he was gorgeous. Maggie agreed. Todd was well mannered and called Dev, sir. Dev planned to get Todd drunk and drop him off Central Pier before the evening ended.

In a quiet moment, Frank had the three in a corner and they toasted one another. Frank had news. "Trentino's gorilla, Karl, has been officially charged with attempted murder with a weapon and is in the slammer awaiting trial. The coroner's report on Little Vinnie is something that should interest you, Bobby. According to the autopsy, his lungs were filled with water and drowning was the cause of death. Not the harpoon. It's not your fault he never learned how to swim. I mean, with a harpoon in his chest. So, officially, I'm telling Danny your mortal soul is still intact."

Devlin smiled and raised his glass.

The evening was filled with dancing, laughter and

countless toasts to Sara's birthday and happiness. The lovely party was coming to a close and Sara announced a toast of her own. The band played a fanfare, the glasses were filled and raised high.

"Thank you all for coming. I'm not used to this public speaking, but this is from my heart. To my old friends. To my new life. And to my new parents."

There wasn't a dry eye in the room.

The closing took place the next day at the offices of Stern, Bradford and Altschuler in the Colonial Room. Edward Bradford represented Emzee Hotel Holdings. Addison Grant Medford III, was no longer with the firm. Oliver Stern, the senior partner, had notified Medford his behavior was not up to SBA standards. Implications that Medford's relationship with the deceased, and now infamous, Vincenzo Trentino, were too intimate and might stain the unsullied escutcheon of the firm. The very efficient Ms. Walsh, however, had been transferred to Mr. Stern's office.

The Max did not attend. He was busy with other matters and knew that he was well represented by counsel, and this was not news worthy. All the attorneys were well prepared and the closing went smoothly. Expenses, a reserve of seven million dollars for Federal and New Jersey taxes, normal closing costs, legal fees, and a million to Jonathan Crandall for his sign-off on any possible claims he might have, reduced the net proceeds of sale remaining for Sara to twelve million. Aside from a very minor sum of two thousand in cash that Devlin had requested be given to Sara at the closing, the proceeds were wired to a special account in Sara's name at Franklin Trust. Congratulations and goodbyes were made, and they headed back to The Palace in Zeist's limo. When they were comfortably settled, Sara had made some decisions that she wanted to share with them.

"I decided on going to U. of P. Not just because it's

closer, Mag. They've got a great law school. It's something I've been thinking about and today made it seem even more appealing. I took two night courses at Stockton College. One in accounting and one in law." Her parents continued to be surprised by her accomplishments and watched in admiration as she thumbed through the large legal envelope Sara had brought along to the closing. She extracted two pages of legal paper, covered with comments and rows of numbers. Sara cleared her throat, a serious demeanor commanded her lovely face and they were respectfully attentive as she spoke.

"Now listen, you guys. I am now of legal age and no vote is necessary for my decision. Which is. . . irremote? . . . No! Irrevocable! I have twelve million in my account at Franklin Trust. That can be invested, very conservatively, at six percent and will bring me in – here, I got it, seven hundred twenty thousand dollars a year. Not bad, huh. I am hiring you two, on a five year contract, to see if you behave, to administer my affairs. You will each receive an annual consulting fee of one hundred and ten thousand dollar, each. Oh, I already said 'each.' "

Maggie was wide eyed at her daughter and Dev attempted to speak, but Sara wagged her finger and stopped him.

"I'm not finished, Dad."

That stopped him.

"That leaves *me* the even sum of five hundred thousand. Or, as Little Vinnie would say, a half a mill. I like round figures." She sat back and smiled like the Cheshire cat. "Okay, now either one of you can speak."

They couldn't. They were speechless. They had produced an irresistible creature more overpowering than Dr. Frankenstein's.

The next morning they were packing to leave The Palace. The TV was on and the mention of Maxwell Zeist brought them all running to view the screen. Interest in Sara, beautiful young heiress, who barely escaped with her life, had captured the attention of the national media. Max's publicist fanned the fire for all it was worth. Soon it would be as stale as old fish. Chet Blakely's voice filled the room.

"Maxwell 'The Max' Zeist has not lost his Midas touch. Completion of a two hundred million dollar financing has been reported by the Zeist organization and promises more jobs and new construction in Atlantic City. Way to go Max."

Dev applauded. "He's unbelievable. Drop him out the window of this suite and he'll land on his feet, just like a cat. Sara, still got the two thousand in cash ?"

Sara nodded.

"Do you remember I taught you how to shoot crap when we were at Lennie Karp's house?"

She nodded again.

"Whattya say we take five hundred, go down to the crap table and get some of Max's two hundred million?"

Sara checked with Maggie. "Don't look at me! If your father wants to teach you his bad habits, it's your decision." Sara seemed uncertain. "I'm kidding, let's get him," said Maggie.

Dev still had a rush coming into the casino, but the presence of the girls at his side calmed him. He spotted his numero uno table at this casino. Only two players? Maybe it was cold. Nah, today had to be lucky. And his favorite duo were working it.

Stan was in the box and Billy Pierce was working the stick. Billy spotted him and his face lit in a black angelic grin.

"Devlin, my man. Ain't seen you in a month. Where you been? You ain't wearing your lucky jacket today."

Dev brought Maggie and Sara to the table rail. "Billy, when you got lucky charms like these two, you don't need old haberdashery."

Devlin's friend, Lorraine, had been filling out a

marker for a player across the pit. Her head perked up at the sound of Devlin's name. She finished her chore, brushed back her hair and strolled over. She and Devlin made eye contact. His eyes tilted to Maggie. Lorraine pouted and discreetly drifted away.

"Okay, Sara, your bankroll is two thousand, but all we're going for is a maximum of twenty-five percent."

Sara quickly responded. "That's five hundred." She peeled it off and dropped it on the table. Chips were pushed to her. She counted them. Her turn was coming to shoot the dice. She checked with her mentor. "Should I put it all on the pass line, or save some for the numbers and the odds ?"

Dev nudged Maggie. Boy, is this kid a fast learner. "Put ten percent, right, fifty dollars, on the pass line and you'll have plenty left for odds and the rest."

Sara furrowed her brow in thought. "I made a lot of money this week, I'm going for a hundred."

She rolled the dice smoothly and watched them land against the back wall. Billy moved the marker to the ten. "Ten, ten, the point is ten. Anybody for the hard ten?"

Sara deftly counted the money in her rack, took double odds for two hundred, fifty each on the four, five and nine and reduced her bankroll to fifty dollars. She got the dice from Billy, rolled a six, collected nothing and then sevened out. Billy chanted the litany and they took her money.

"Hey, Dev," said Billy, "she is very pretty, but she shoots crap like you shoot basketball."

They all laughed, Sara the hardest. "I've still got fifty left. You want to try to do it, Maggie?" Maggie shook her head. "How about you, Dev?"

"Nah, leave it for the boys." Billy gave them another of his beautiful smiles for a thank you. For the first time in his life, Devlin turned down an offer to shoot crap with some one else bankrolling him. He hugged Sara. "You got that out of your system in a hurry. I've got a good idea. We've been cooped up for weeks, let's walk on the boardwalk and get some sunshine. And don't be upset you lost,

Sara. You win some, you lose some."

"I'm not upset. I've still got eleven million, nine hundred ninety nine thousand, five hundred left."

"Come with me, ladies," said Dev, "I know a guy named Murray Kleinerman who makes the best salt water taffy that ever ruined your teeth."

They left the neon lit rooms for the bright sunshine outdoors.

Heads turned to admire the sight of Dev in the middle, his arms around the shoulders of his two beauties as they trod the grey boards.